'I don't like being pushed around.'

'You seem to do the shoving,' he said.

'Any objections? Not that it's any of your business.'

'None at all,' Ivan agreed cheerfully. 'You're beautiful enough to almost get away with murder, so long as you stay with the wimps. But watch out that one of the other sort never gets you in his sights.'

Alice found herself backing as he smiled down into her suddenly frightened face.

Dear Reader

Well, summer is almost upon us. Time to think about holidays, perhaps? Where to go? What to do? And how to get everything you own into one suitcase! Wherever you decide to go, don't forget to pack plenty of Mills & Boon novels. This month's selection includes such exotic locations as Andalucía, Brazil and the Aegean Islands, so you can enjoy lots of holiday romance even if you stay at home!

The Editor

Jane Donnelly began earning her living as a writer as a teenage reporter. When she married the editor of the newspaper she freelanced for women's mags for a while, and wrote her first Mills & Boon romance as a hard-up single parent. Now she lives in a roses-round-the-door cottage near Stratford upon Avon, with her daughter, four dogs and assorted rescued animals. Besides writing she enjoys travelling, swimming, walking and the company of friends.

SHADOW OF
A TIGER

BY

JANE DONNELLY

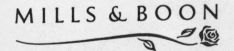

MILLS & BOON LIMITED
ETON HOUSE, 18-24 PARADISE ROAD
RICHMOND, SURREY TW9 1SR

*First published in Great Britain 1994
by Mills & Boon Limited*

© Jane Donnelly 1994

*Australian copyright 1994
Philippine copyright 1994
This edition 1994*

ISBN 0 263 78510 6

*Set in Times Roman 10½ on 12 pt.
01-9406-51086 C*

Made and printed in Great Britain

CHAPTER ONE

'CAN I come in for a coffee?' he asked, getting her case out of the boot of his car, and she said,

'Not tonight, I'm dead-beat; I'm just going to drop everything and fall into bed,' and thought wryly that she might have put that better, although a sense of humour had never been Martin's strong point.

But he was considerate, and Alice looked tired after the long journey. The lamplight gave her pale skin a translucent sheen and shadowed her eyes. 'It was a good holiday, wasn't it?' he said, and he kissed her gently. 'See you tomorrow.'

She said yes to both and smiled for him and let herself into the house, and heard his car drive away as she walked down the black and white tiled hall, past the door painted white with the stark design of a huge black question mark, through the plain white door next to it, and into the good-sized high-ceilinged room that had been her bed-sit for the last three years.

It was a relief to be home. The familiarity of the place comforted her. It had been a good holiday. Martin Royston's family, including his brother's wife and his sister's fiancé, had all welcomed Alice, and the Roystons' Florida villa had been super in every way.

Alice and Martin had only been able to get away from work for a fortnight, but by the middle of the first week she had known there were problems ahead. Since they'd met at a party four months before she had been going around with Martin. They had what she considered a very satisfactory relationship, but she had been a fool to imagine it could continue unchanged indefinitely.

That was because she hadn't thought about the future at all. Stupid, perhaps, but she valued her independence, and he had seemed to accept that, even admire it. Apart from her looks—she was a cool and classy blonde with a good bone-structure and a model-girl's height—her self-assurance and laid-back attitude had intrigued him from the start.

And at some stage his mother must have decided that Alice Ashby was a suitable partner for an up-and-coming accountant, because Patrica Royston had introduced her to friends in adjoining villas, with a coy little smile, as, 'My son Martin's Alice.'

That had given Alice a jolt. She had not cared for the sound of that. She had met his parents before, and his sister, but here all the family were gathered together, all assuming that she and Martin were as good as engaged. Martin, it seemed, was ready to take on a wife, but Alice did not want a husband.

She wanted a friend, a companion, a lover, but she was giving nobody legal rights over her. Martin was as close as he was getting. It had been a good holiday, because they were nice folk, and she was their guest, and there was no call for high drama, embarrassing everybody.

Now she was home again she would get back into the routine of work first then play, and hope that Martin would take no for an answer next time. Better still, that there wouldn't be a next time.

'When we're married...' he had said one afternoon when the talk around the pool was on houses and the superior residences being built backing on to the golf course at home. His sister and her fiancé had one earmarked. 'When we're married,' Martin said, 'something like that might suit us.'

Alice had opened her mouth to say, It wouldn't suit me. I'm very well suited as I am: single and staying that way. But everyone was relaxed, basking in the sunshine, at peace with the world, and they had been so kind to her that it had seemed ungracious to blurt out, I don't want to be part of your family; I'd rather stay on my own.

So she had waited until she had Martin more or less alone, swimming in the pool a few minutes later, and then she had said, 'I'm not marrying you, you know; I'm not marrying anybody.'

The sun had reddened his fairish complexion in spite of the suntan oil, while Alice, who had long ago learned to rely on the protection of a wide-brimmed hat, had a skin like porcelain. With the water foaming around her as she did a leisurely backstroke she looked, he thought, as flawless and beautiful as a water nymph. 'All right,' he said. 'All right.'

Whether it would be all right remained to be seen. He had not mentioned marriage again, and now the holiday was over Alice hoped that their no-strings understanding would continue, because she really was very fond of Martin.

Most of the time she thought she was in love with him, but she always knew that she hated the idea of total surrender to any man. She had to keep the power to say no. She needed space, and time alone, and right now she needed a good night's sleep.

She was tired, but getting out of her travelling clothes, cleansing off her make-up and standing under a tepid shower still left her mind ticking at a restless rate. Barefoot, in blue and white men's pyjamas, with trousers and sleeves rolled up, she went into the kitchen and switched on the kettle.

A hot drink might help. Not coffee; caffeine wouldn't do her any good. Something milky and malty, except she had no milk until tomorrow. Tea without milk probably kept you awake too. But the clock on the wall had not yet reached ten, and there had been a light on upstairs, so Eleanor was still up.

She would have milk. It was a wonder she hadn't come down before now, unless she thought Alice had brought Martin in with her and was being tactful. Eleanor approved of Martin. 'A nice young man, dear—steady and reliable,' Eleanor Pringle had pronounced, with the character assessment experience of thirty years' schoolteaching behind her.

Eleanor would want to hear about the holiday, but she was all for girls having careers, and Alice could tell her about the marriage crisis without being warned that she was missing out on an eligible husband. Eleanor would be sensible without being bossy, and a quiet natter could soothe Alice's tension away.

A carpeted staircase led up from the hall to a door that was always open. Beyond that was Miss Pringle's self-contained apartment. The room plan was identical to the ground floor, but over Alice's bed-sitter was Eleanor's living-room, where in the evenings she usually sat reading, watching television or listening to music.

Alice went from the lighted corridor into the room where the radio was playing and a side-lamp burned. 'I'm back,' she said brightly, and blinked in the dimmer light, and saw the figure in the window.

The blood drained from her face, leaving it cold, clammy and white. In total shock she could neither speak nor move. It could only have been seconds before the man spoke, but if he had not she could have stayed frozen, hypnotised, until she slumped unconscious.

'Hello,' he said. He was very tall, very broad-shouldered. There was light now to see his face, but he was still a dark shape to her. 'Are you all right?' he asked, and she had to be paler than death.

'Where's Miss Pringle?' That was her voice, tiny, tinny.

'Sorry, I don't know.' She had thought she would always remember and recognise his voice, but now she couldn't be sure. 'I'm her lodger,' he said. 'On a six-month lease.'

She knew Eleanor was trying to sell, although this was the first she had heard about renting. Somehow she managed to say, 'I came up to borrow some milk, but it doesn't matter; don't bother.' Then she edged away to the door at the top of the stairs and closed it behind her, although as it didn't lock on either side there was no point in that.

Downstairs, in her living-room, the blood was rushing back, roaring in her ears, and she clenched her hands into tight fists, whispering, 'I'm all right; I'm just fine. Nothing happened to me—nothing at all.'

Of course nothing had. Except that there was a stranger upstairs who probably had every right to be there. He had nearly scared the life out of her because she had not expected him and because he was standing by the window, and who the hell was he?

Surely Eleanor would not vanish without leaving a
warning that she had installed a tenant and saying
how Alice could contact her? There had to be a
message. Most likely in the office. Eleanor had had
the spare downstairs keys, and Alice opened the dividing door between this room, which opened on to
the garden, and the front room that overlooked the
street.

The front room was her workplace, and on her
desk, propped up against the in-tray containing the
last two weeks' mail, was a folded piece of paper with
'Alice' written in Eleanor's neat distinctive script.

The note was brief...

> Leaving you with a very interesting lodger. I'll
> let him tell you how he makes a living. You two
> might get together. Love Eleanor

And there a phone number.

So it was legal and above-board. Nothing sinister
at all. She had been tired and ever so slightly worried
about Martin, and her mind had played time-warp
tricks. But now she was over her panic, and when she
heard the knock on the door it was the self-possessed
Alice whom all her friends would have recognised who
went to answer it, half expecting to see a man with a
bottle of milk out there.

He was empty-handed, so that was not the reason
he was here. 'Was I that much of a shock?' he asked.
He must have been well over six feet and long and
lean: long nose, long mouth, long pugnacious jaw.
He was watching her closely.

As she had turned white as a sheet and staggered
away when she set eyes on him he must be wondering

what ailed her, and she stammered, 'It was a shock; I didn't know Miss Pringle had moved out.'

'What did you think had moved in—a ghost?'

A shiver ran through her and she started to talk fast. 'Put it down to jet-lag. I've just flown in from Florida and I almost sleep-walked upstairs. I hadn't found her note then.'

She was still clutching it and she glanced down. 'By the way, what do you do for a living? She says here that I should ask you.'

He shrugged broad shoulders. 'Bit of this, bit of that. Right now I'm putting a book together.'

She waved the note. 'So that's what she means by saying we might get together. I've edited a charity book and I've ghosted memoirs, that sort of thing.'

She ran a one-woman public relations business, although why she was producing her credentials for him she did not know. All the same, she added, 'They've done quite well locally.'

'Good,' he said, 'but hardly my line of country. I'll say goodnight. They tell me rest's the thing for jet-lag.'

As he reached the staircase she asked, 'Have we come across each other before?'

'No,' he said flatly, but how could anyone be that certain? If he thought not, surely the natural answer was, I don't think so.

He closed the door at the top of the stairs behind him and she stepped into the hall to switch off the light down here. She locked her doors, and got into the divan bed she had left made up and ready for her late return, and sat upright, her hands clasped around her ankles, her heart pounding against her ribcage.

Had they met before? Oh, lord, she prayed, don't let him be the one. But that room upstairs was haunted. Four years ago it had been her bedroom. Her mother had died when Alice was in her early teens, and when she was eighteen this had still been a family house for herself and her father.

One warm summer night she had woken and seen the shape at the window, and before she could scream it was on her. She was gagged and tied, swiftly and brutally, and when she struggled the hands on her throat tightened, nearly throttling her, until she lay choking and unresisting.

Theft was his main objective. He left her, staked out on the bed, and she heard him moving through the house. She was alone. The grandfather clock struck in the hall and she knew it would be hours before her father returned from his weekly poker sessions at the press club.

Long before then the man in black and Balaclava would come back to do what he liked with her. Her flimsy nightgown was torn, she was naked and pinned down, and if she tried to fight him he would kill her.

She wanted to live. Nothing mattered more than staying alive. She would do anything not to die here in the dark at the hands of a rapist, anything he told her to do.

So she waited, her ears magnifying every sound, her skin shrivelling as though she were packed in ice, and her brain on fire.

She was an only child. Her mother had been an invalid for years before she died, so that Alice had always been practical for her age. But, beneath her composure, there was an imagination so vivid that

she could escape into another world whenever this one
became dull or lonely.

It made her a brilliant English student and a sym-
pathetic friend. 'You understand how I feel,' her
friends would say, and that night Alice imagined what
was going to happen to her in savage and agonising
detail. The initial outrage of being bound and gagged
and the tearing degradation that would follow were
both as real to her as though both had happened
already.

She was violated in every way before she saw him
again. When he dropped the bag he was carrying, and
came shambling towards the bed, she was drained of
strength. If he produced a knife she would be
powerless to strain away from it.

She was not praying. Her mind was too deranged
with terror for any coherent thought, but what happened next was a little miracle: a burst of voices and
laughter from downstairs, the masked man stopping,
hunched and listening, then grabbing the bag and
climbing out of the open window into the thick,
twisted boughs of the creeper that covered that side
of the house.

She saw him framed in the window as he spoke to
her for the first time, then there was nothing out there
but the night sky, in here an empty room, and the
blessed voices below.

She couldn't move or call. Her feet were tied
together, her wrists were lashed to the bedposts, and
a gag cut cruelly across her mouth. The hall light from
downstairs shone through her open door and the
voices suddenly went silent.

Then her father roared her name—'Alice, *Alice*,'—
and she heard him running up the stairs. When he

rushed into her room two other men were behind him, and the light was on, and her father's face was grey and his lips were blue, and he kept sobbing her name while they cut her loose and wrapped her in a coverlet and eased the gag out of her mouth.

She thought her mouth was cut and bleeding, it ached so. But that was only bruising from the tightness of the gag, and she had to tell him she was all right, because he sounded out of his mind and his heart was not strong. 'I'm all right,' she croaked. 'I'm just fine. Nothing happened to me, nothing at all.'

It seemed that way. The sneak-thief had taken a number of portable things: bric-à-brac, silverware, jewellery, money and credit cards from a bureau. It was seeing the drawers tumbled out that had alerted her father and his friends to the break-in.

The thief had gagged and bound Alice, but that was all, and their friends could hardly believe the thousand-to-one chance that had caused a power cut at the press club and brought her father and his cronies to her rescue in the nick of time.

She had been incredibly lucky, although the thief had got away with the loot. Her description of a masked man was not much use. The list of stolen goods was circulated, but as break-ins went this was minor, and nothing that could be identified turned up, and if he was ever arrested it was not for that night's work.

For a while Alice was quite a heroine. When they found her it was her father who went to pieces and Alice who reassured them that she was all right. Everyone admired her cool courage, and her closest friends said they bet she would have talked her way out of it if help had not come, that Alice would never have panicked, because she never did, but of course it was wonderful that she had escaped with nothing worse than a few bruises.

She could have told them that from the moment those gloved hands seized her she had been reduced to something less than human. The bruises would fade within weeks, but the memory of terror might never leave her. Only she told this to no one.

The old-fashioned sash-cord windows were replaced by modern double glazing and thief-proof locks. Alice moved bedrooms and chose another room with a different outlook, so that she would never again wake in the night facing the window where she had seen the man.

The wistaria was hacked to the ground. She came home from day college one afternoon soon after the break-in to find them at work on it, the lawn covered with ripped-out creeper and trampled blossoms. It had been a spectacular sight every year, masses of purple flowers cascading down, but, as the police pointed out, it was like leaving ladders to every upper window, and her father had immediately ordered a drastic pruning.

It had to be done, but the destruction chilled her. She was sure it would never bloom again; the sawn-off boughs that were left looked raw and stunted. Now, four years later, there were a few runners from old roots, but the plant had never recovered. Each winter she expected the frost to finish it.

In those years life had changed in some ways for her. She had lost her father; she now ran what had been his business. She would always miss him—she had loved him dearly—but from the night of the break-in she had had a phobia against losing control.

She was coping well with her life and her work, and the only thing that really scared her was the idea of ever being helpless again, in someone else's power.

Now she made herself relax, because she must be clear-headed in the morning to deal with the backlog she had not organised ahead when she went on holiday. How stupid to jump at shadows and let the nightmare crawl back. Go to sleep, she ordered herself; you're going to have enough on your hands with work and with Martin without conjuring up imaginary horrors.

She was tired, and her bed felt right, and everything around her was where and how it should be, and within a few minutes she was sound asleep.

It was a pity about Eleanor. When she was left on her own Alice had had the detached Victorian house converted, and Eleanor Pringle had bought the upstairs apartment. She and Alice had got along famously, but when she retired she had decided to join her sister in Australia, starting a new life in her sixties, and put her property on the market again.

It had been waiting for a buyer for months, and Alice had hoped that Eleanor was going off the idea, because she liked having her here, being able to run upstairs to swap gossip and share a coffee and a Danish pastry, or a glass or two of wine if the mood took them.

She was fond of Eleanor, who was utterly trust-worthy, but now there was a stranger under the roof she would want her front door key handed back, and a bolt on the door at the top of the stairs, because the first-floor entrance was by an iron staircase at the back of the house; there was no right of way through Alice's hall.

This morning she decided she had no interest in the lodger at all. She was used to men taking an interest in her. She was often asked, 'Has anyone ever told you you look like...?' and named some stunning and sexy actress or singer, and she always laughed and said, 'I should be so lucky,' knowing how little she had in common with them.

She surely did not want that man upstairs fancying her. That would be a terrible nuisance; it didn't bear thinking of. She switched on the coffee percolator and shivered and remembered the old saying, 'Somebody's walking over my grave.'

Leaving the coffee to percolate, she collected the morning mail from the box behind the front door and took it into the office.

There was a phone bill she had been expecting, some junk mail and three business letters. With those in the in-tray that Eleanor had been piling up for her, she was going to be busy. She wouldn't phone Eleanor yet; it was early and she was in no hurry to hear about the lodger. She didn't give a damn about him. These were separate apartments; she need see no more of him than she did of her other neighbours.

She glanced through the mail, then opened her desk diary and reached to switch on the answerphone, when she saw him in the doorway. He startled her, because she hadn't heard him coming in on the tiled floor of the hall, but she had been occupied, with work on her mind.

'You wanted this?' he said. He had a bottle of milk.

'Yes. Thanks.' There was something familiar about him. Nothing to do with the sneak-thief; his face had been covered. But this was a face you wouldn't forget in a hurry, and she felt that she might have seen it before.

She got up and he said, 'How about a trade? Coffee for milk.'

The rich roasted aroma met her in the hall as she went into the kitchen, and he followed as far as that doorway. 'You've got milk and no coffee?' she said.

'I'm not very well equipped; I only moved in yesterday. I met a milk-float while I was out walking, but I didn't find a coffee-shop open.' He must walk early through almost empty streets, and she could hardly refuse the swap.

She took down two mugs from a collection. She searched for odd and attractive mugs in boot fairs and junk shops, and now she poured into one with gilded hearts linked by daisy chains, and into a coronation mug of George VI and Elizabeth, his queen.

'Milk? Sugar?' she asked.

'Neither, thanks.'

'You don't take milk? Then this *was* neighbourly.'

She did not want him being neighbourly. She wanted him keeping to his own apartment and out of hers, and later she would bring up the matter of the front door key. But while she was tipping his milk into her coffee hardly seemed the time.

She intended drinking hers at her desk, so she was not inviting him to sit down, and as he took the coronation mug he asked, 'Does that mean anything in particular?' indicating the big black question mark on the white office door.

She explained, 'My father chose it. This is a publicity consultancy.'

'I saw the plaque—"Clive Ashby, Media and Marketing".'

A brass plate was on the wall by the front door. She had kept the name; it was known and respected in the town. She said, 'When he started he wanted something eye-catching as a logo, and he chose a query.'

'Very baffling.' That was the idea. It made folk look twice when they saw it on the car, or on ads, and they remembered it. 'So what's the answer?' he asked.

'Different questions, different answers.'

'A man with all the answers. I look forward to meeting him.'

'You might have to wait some time. He died.' She kept her voice steady, but it would always hurt to say, He died. 'I'm Alice Ashby.'

'I'm sorry.' From a stranger that was just a cliché. He introduced himself. 'Ivan Blackmore.'

She knew that name. She *had* seen that face—on book jackets, in magazines. She had read none of his books, but plenty of others had. They were successful thrillers, and she said drily, 'Miss Partridge was wrong, thinking you'd need a ghost writer. Have you met her?'

'Briefly.'

·Well, she's a retired headmistress and a great reader, but, as you said earlier, not in your line of country. Neither am I, I'm afraid; I haven't read you either. Thank you for the milk; may I pay you?'

'It was a trade.'

'Thanks again; I have to get to work.' She couldn't expect him to gulp down the scalding coffee, but she wasn't standing here chatting. 'Excuse me,' she said, and went back into the office, closing the door behind her.

A couple of minutes later she looked out into the hall, across to the kitchen. He had gone, and the door at the top of the stairs was closed. Until she fitted a bolt that would keep nobody out, but she had felt restless while he could have been in her kitchen.

Now she got down to work, making notes of messages on the answerphone, refreshing her memory for today in the diary. Her first appointment was twelve o'clock, and she drafted a couple of letters to clients, then caught herself sitting quite still and listening.

These houses were solidly built. Down here you couldn't hear anyone upstairs unless they were shifting heavy furniture or had a music centre on full-blast. That night she had heard every footfall because doors had been open and she had been as alert as a trapped animal.

Eleanor's lodger would be moving around up there now and Alice couldn't hear a thing, and she must stop harking back, because there was no link between him and the robber of four years ago. If her first sight of Blackmore had not been in half-light at that window the idea would never have entered her head. She was almost sure it would not.

Her phone rang and a chirpy voice said, 'Alice? Oh, good, you're home. It's Ros here. Have a good time?'

'Mmm,' said Alice.

'What was the villa like?'

'It was really something.'

Ros sighed. 'I could do with a spell in Florida this time of year; I hate February. Were you surprised to find Miss Pringle gone? Oh, and we've got your keys; she left them with us.'

Ros worked for the estate agents who were handling the sale of Eleanor's apartment. She and Alice had known each other all their lives, and right from primary school Ros had been rattling away like marbles in an empty can. She went on now, hardly drawing breath.

'What about the tenant we found for her? Isn't he the most gorgeous hunk you ever saw?' Not by a very long way, thought Alice.

'*And* he's famous,' Ros went on triumphantly. 'Well, sort of. Did you know that? He writes thrillers. Well, you know we haven't had much luck selling the apartment, and renting it seemed a good idea, because when she gets out to Australia she might find she doesn't get on all that well with her sister after all these years, and this way she'll have a home to come back to if she wants to, and meantime it's earning her good money.'

'So it is,' said Alice. 'How did you find him?'

'Seems he was looking for somewhere to stay round here. He saw the photograph for your house in the window and came in and asked about it and if a lease would be considered, and it went through just like that.'

He wanted this town, but it was crazy to think he might have wanted this house. 'I'll call in for the keys,' Alice said.

'I suppose you and Martin didn't get engaged or anything while you were living it up in Florida?' asked Ros.

'You suppose right,' said Alice.

She collected her keys when she came out of the local newspaper offices, where she had been discussing layouts in the advertising department, then she went into the public library and looked up Blackmore, Ivan.

Half a dozen books were listed, but there was only one on the shelves. His photograph was inside the back cover: head and shoulders, roll-neck sweater, unsmiling, hooded eyes unreadable. The thick, unruly hair curled very slightly behind the ears—tidied up for the camera, probably. Two months without a good haircut, she thought, and he'd pass for a wild man.

She took the book out, and when she let herself into her office she saw him again, through the far window in the garden. He *was* beginning to haunt her. What she should do now was close the dividing door and get on with her work, but instead she found herself walking through her bed-sit and opening the long French windows.

Enclosed in a copper beech hedge, it was a big garden, and the only way she could cope with it was to let the grass grow between the trees and pay someone to go up and down with the mower during the summer months. Crocuses were bursting through here and there, and the effect was pleasantly casual.

He had passed her window and now he was at the corner of the house. When she stepped out he turned and waited. As she reached him she cleared her throat. 'You do understand about the garden?'

'What about it?'

'It's mine. I mean, it doesn't go with the upstairs apartment. You have right of way round the side and on the patio——' which was three flagstones wide

'—because your entrance goes up from there. But we don't share the garden.'

Eleanor had sat on the seat under the horse-chestnut tree on many a warm afternoon, sometimes alone, sometimes taking tea with her friends. She had used the garden far more than Alice had, but Alice was not ceding any territory to him, although she realised how petty she was sounding when he said, 'You should put up a notice—"Keep off My Grass". What do you think I might be doing out here? Holding orgies? A small, select acid party?'

'Don't be absurd,' she said coldly.

'So what's your worry?' He looked around. 'Hardly Kew Gardens, is it? I've walked across better-kept fields.' Winter had roughened the grass; when there were straight-cut lines from a professional mowing it would look better.

Her worry was that she did not want him where she could see him from her window, but that was hard to explain, and she said stubbornly, 'Legally the garden is mine.'

'And you know your rights.'

'Yes, I do.'

'Perhaps it's as well you didn't put up a "Keep Off" notice; the challenge might have been too much.'

She knew he was laughing at her, although he was hardly smiling, and she said impulsively, 'When you see "Keep Out" do you have to break in?' and her breath caught in her throat.

He smiled then, a quick flash of white teeth. His eyes, as dark as his hair, seemed to flash too, and it was a loaded question to ask any man even if he was a law-abiding citizen. 'Not every time,' he said.

From where they were standing they could see the side of the house where the wistaria had grown, and a compulsion kept her chattering. 'The wistaria used to be like a great purple waterfall on this wall in summer.'

'So why cut it down?'

Some of the metal anchoring pegs had been left in, reaching higher than the room that had been her bedroom. He seemed to be looking up at that window now, and she could have said, Because we were robbed and I was attacked one night when a man climbed in that way. But she couldn't get those words out and she said instead, 'My father decided it was crumbling the brickwork.'

'A pity.'

'Yes, well . . .' She turned away. 'Of course I don't object to you using the garden so long as you remember it isn't your land.'

'If I get the urge to commune with nature by walking round a tree I'll take you up on that,' he said, 'but I don't do much communing.'

She was sounding so pompous over an unkempt half-acre of grass, so she said tritely, 'Suit yourself,' and went back into the house, her long legs covering the ground in long strides.

This time she did close the dividing door, shutting the office off from the French windows. Eleanor's tenant might turn out to be a model lodger, but so far Alice did not like him at all. Something about him disturbed her so much that she had to put his book away in a drawer before she could get on with her work.

Until her midday appointment she concentrated on phone calls and mail, and when the doorbell rang around twelve she was in good form again. Work could do that for her—give her spirits a lift. She often hit snags—PR was a chancy business—but she got on well with most of her clients because she had flair and she worked hard for them.

The holiday had been her first real break in years and, in spite of the misunderstanding with Martin's family, she was feeling the benefit of all that relaxation and sunshine and good food. She opened the front door, smiling, and the young woman on the doorstep grinned back.

Graduating from a market stall, this client was opening a shop in the new precinct tomorrow, and Alice had arranged publicity. The adverts were all out, a local beauty queen was cutting the ribbon, and punch and cookies were being provided.

Patsy and Alice went over the details again, and everything seemed in hand. Alice would be along with a photographer, and Patsy said goodbye after spending half an hour giggling with excitement and nerves.

At her desk Alice opened a drawer, and her happy mood vanished like a puff of smoke as she took the book out again.

She opened it at random, reading a page. The pace was fast and it was written well enough to grab even someone dipping into it, as she was. Immediately you were hooked; you wanted to know what was going on with these folk.

There was no 'About the author' under the photograph, just the name, and on the back cover some critical quotes—all praising it, of course; the publishers wouldn't be using them if they weren't. One, from a national quality newspaper, said,

A powerful and troubling writer. It is hard to believe that Blackmore has not lived through the situations he describes.

So there should be some clues in here to the kind of man he was, and she had to dig for them. She could keep telling herself there was no connection between him and the masked man, but without proof, one way or the other, the doubts could grow and fester.

Because as long as she lived she would never forget what the intruder had said in the open window of her room—words that had stayed in her mind ever since . . . 'I'll be back . . .'

CHAPTER TWO

ALICE tried the phone number Eleanor Pringle had left on her note, and it rang for a while, but there was no reply. It was a Bath number. Eleanor's married niece lived in Bath, so that would be where Eleanor was staying, and Alice would try again later.

If they had only met briefly, Eleanor was not going to be able to tell her much about the Blackmore character, but she had been a good friend while they shared this house and Alice wanted to speak to her again before she took flight across the world, just to say goodbye and wish her well.

'Leaving you with a very interesting lodger,' Eleanor's note read, which made Alice wince, because interesting was not the half of it. At best he was maddeningly intrusive. At worst . . . But she wouldn't think about that because of course that couldn't be happening.

When there was a tap on the door, which opened immediately, and there he was, she was not surprised. Nobody else could get in with the front door closed, but after the scene in the garden she hesitated about declaring the hall a no-go area. She would be sounding paranoid about her privacy, which in a way she was.

'I've put your mug in the kitchen,' he said.

'Right.'

'What do you do about lunch?'

She was sitting here in an empty room at lunchtime, and before she could say she was carrying on working, or that she had a business date, he had noticed his book on her desk. He could hardly miss it right there in front of her, and she didn't want him asking how she had come by it, didn't want to have to admit she had dashed round to the library to get it out. But she had to say something about it, and she indicated the critics' quotes and said, 'You've got some fans.'

'You should have seen the ones they didn't print.' He was probably joking; it wasn't easy to tell.

'Do you get bad reviews?'

'Everybody doesn't love me.'

He looked amused, not bothered, and she muttered, 'I can believe that.'

'Come and eat,' he tempted her, 'and I'll tell you the plot and save you the trouble of reading it.' She had to smile, and he said approvingly, 'That's better; the chill was getting to my bones.'

She had been behaving stupidly. Of course he wasn't the burglar, nor was he Jack the Ripper, but she had been carrying on as if he were. And what the heck, why not share a sandwich or whatever? 'All right,' she said.

She turned on the answerphone and collected a camel trench coat and a scarlet shawl and asked, 'What kind of eating place do you want?'

'What do you have?'

She rattled them off. 'Traditional English, pizza parlour, Chinese, Indian, fish and chips.'

'Do you do the PR for the tourist board?'

'No, I've just always lived here.' She pulled the heavy front door to behind them. The brass plaque needed cleaning. She gave it a weekly rub-up, and it had tarnished while she was on holiday. She resisted the urge now to attack it with a tissue and asked, 'Where do you come from?'

'Cornwall.'

He didn't say which town, and after a few seconds she said, 'Have you always lived there?'

'No.' He answered amiably, but he didn't elaborate, and she tried another tack.

'Why are you here now? Why our town?'

'If you've never wanted to leave you must feel it's worth spending six months here.'

'Yes, but...'

This was not a holiday resort. Not a beauty spot. It was a busy little Midlands town in what had once been a coal-mining area, and now had a golf course, farms and forestry plantations on the open country. And in the town there were industries, shops and offices. 'Have you friends here?'

She supposed she was probing now, but again he just said, 'No,' so it was obvious he wasn't going to talk about himself. She didn't care. She would prefer a quiet lunch hour to putting herself out to make small talk, although she did wonder why he had bothered getting her to join him. On the pavement he asked, 'Do we take a car?'

Hers was in the garage here. Eleanor had had a lock-up just round the corner, so he probably had a car there, but Alice said, 'I was going to eat in the precinct; that's where I've got to be this afternoon. It's only ten minutes' walk, and parking can be awkward.'

'Sounds fine,' he said, and she set off with him down the wide tree-lined road.

The sun was out and early spring flowers brightened front gardens. Her two weeks away had made a

difference, and she would be enjoying this short stroll
into town more if she had been alone, but she was so
conscious of the man beside her that nothing else
really registered.

He moved with a loose-limbed athlete's stride, a
big man who would be light and quick on his feet,
and silently she asked, How are you at climbing
creepers, getting into a house through an open
window? And then—*Stop that*! And because she could
feel that he was looking at her she said the first safe
thing that came into her head. 'Isn't it a lovely day?'

'Pale sunshine after Florida.'

'Of course.' And the breeze was cool enough to
make her pull the shawl around her.

'So are you pale.'

Not as pale as she had gone last night when she
first saw him, but no advertisement for two weeks'
sun-filled holiday. 'I burn,' she said. 'So I slap on the
sun-block and take no chances.'

'Nobody would take you for a chancer.'

It wasn't a compliment, and it was not true. She
took risks—not emotionally, but in all sorts of other
ways. She said tartly, 'You are, of course,' and he
grinned.

'But I don't burn.'

'Must be handy to be flame-proof.' And she smiled
too, because it was a lovely spring day and she was
having lunch with a fairly attractive man whom she
had met yesterday for the first time. No big deal, certainly nothing to get fussed about. 'So we're into
town,' she said as the road ended in a roundabout
and busier streets.

When they reached the shopping precinct he said,
'There've been some changes.'

'Aren't there always? How long since you were here?'

'A few years, just passing through, but there were market stalls here then.'

'This has been open just over a year. The market's in the market hall now, leading off.' She wouldn't ask if he was here four years ago; she wouldn't think about that. She said, 'I was going to the deli. There's a café there.'

The precinct was under cover, and sunlight streamed through high windows. When all the units on the ground floor were taken they might get round to opening the floor above. For now a mural of palm trees, bright yellow beaches and unbelievably blue seas, done by local art students, filled the gaps.

Down below the shop windows were colourful, and a few Monday customers ambled around. The delicatessen was earning a reputation for value-for-money lunches, and most days its half a dozen tables were filled. But Alice often came here on Mondays, and the proprietors greeted her with, 'Had a good holiday?'

She said it had been marvellous, and knew that the wife at least was wondering who the man was—if he was a client or something else. Mrs Taylor came herself to their window table, to take their order and get a closer look at him.

Alice settled for a slice of broccoli and cheese quiche and a green salad, and recommended the baked potatoes with a range of speciality fillings. When they came the salad was prettily presented, but the big potato with chilli con carne looked a heartier meal, and she explained, 'I've been over-eating for a fortnight; I'm into health food for a few days.'

'No sign of spare flesh,' he said. She had slipped her coat and shawl over the back of her chair, but she was wearing a loose, enveloping sweater.

'I could be hiding a lot of extra pounds under this,' she said gaily.

'No, you couldn't,' he said, and she thought, No flab on you, either. He was in a dark grey suit and a thin black sweater, and he was whipcord muscles and sinew on the big frame. She knew that just by looking at him, and she hoped he couldn't 'see' her as clearly through her good thick sweater.

But he was looking through the window, up at the eye-catching mural, and she asked, 'What do you think of that?'

When he raised an eyebrow she grinned. 'I think it's meant to be dreamland. You're down here in a shopping centre and you can look up and dream you're in the South Seas.'

'No South Seas I've ever seen.'

'That's the drawback of having seen it all. I've never been near Hawaii, so it wouldn't surprise me if a troupe of hula dancers came shimmying along in front of it.'

'There's one of them down here,' he said.

'What?'

Patsy's shop unit was opposite, with a streamer announcing, 'Opening Tomorrow, Ten O'Clock', and Patsy, who had just spotted Alice at the window table, was jumping up and down in front and waving.

Alice waved back. 'One of my clients,' she said solemnly. 'She opens tomorrow and she's on a high.'

He waved too, and Patsy gave them a thumbs-up for good luck before she went back into her shop.

'Her family have a market stall,' Alice explained, 'and Patsy is taking some of it up-market. I do the publicity for the stallholders, I handle the adverts, and each week I write a column for the local paper called "Market News".'

It was fun writing, because there was always a human-interest tale to tell, but it was small-town stuff, and she remembered him saying, 'Hardly my line of country' when she had discussed her work before.

She was picking her way through her food. 'Tell me about yourself,' she said, as she would have said to anyone who was almost a stranger sitting with her at lunch.

'I don't need PR.' Of course he didn't, and although he said that with a smile he could be warning her off.

But stubbornly she went on, 'Was the critic right—the one who thought you'd experienced most of the things you write about?'

'A few of them.'

'I'll start reading the book I've got tonight,' she said. 'And don't tell me what it's about; I'll find out for myself.'

She said that lightly, but she looked away from him, because she was not sure herself what she would be looking for in his book, and she didn't want him to start wondering.

They were at the end of the meal, drinking their coffee, and Alice was talking about walks and places around here that were worth seeing, when a waitress put their bill on the table.

She stretched across to take it and so did he, holding her hand away for a moment. What happened on her part was pure reflex. She jerked her fingers back as if they were scalded and then began babbling apologies, because that had almost been as hostile as hitting him across the face.

'I'm sorry,' she stammered. 'You made me jump.'

'Don't read the book after dark, not even with the lights on,' he drawled.

'W-why not?'

'It could give you nightmares. You're a very nervous lady.'

'No, I'm not.'

She had had nightmares afterwards, but not for years, nor was she nervous. Her reaction had been triggered by a deep-down conviction that she would know if her attacker touched her again, she really would know.

The robber had worn rough gloves, and this man's hand was hard and cool. The touch was different; the men were different. She believed that, even if her subconscious was making a fool out of her.

He was studying her across the red and white gingham cloth, and she couldn't blame him if he was coming to the conclusion that she was a borderline nutcase.

He had the little slip of paper that was the bill, and she said, 'I insist on paying my share. I always pay my share.'

'I owe you a lunch at least,' he said. 'I seem to be playing hell with your nervous system.'

She had been crazily on edge, and from now on she would control herself better. She tried to joke, 'Jet-lag seems to leave you twitchy for a few hours, but thanks for lunch.'

'A pleasure.' She supposed it might have been if he didn't mind someone carrying on as if he were a plague carrier, and she stood up, getting into her coat and

shawl, excusing herself for leaving while his cup was
still half full.

'I must go. I have to see about my copy for
Saturday's column.'

'Take it easy,' he said.

'I do.' She was a cool lady. Last night and just now
were entirely out of character.

'You could have fooled me,' he said.

She laughed a little, as if they were both laughing,
and as she went out the waitress asked, 'Everything
all right?'

'Yes.'

'Only I saw you . . .' She gestured a hand jerk. 'Was
it a spider or something?'

'I scratched my hand on something,' Alice invented
wildly, and left the café, crossing the precinct and
entering the market hall without looking back.

She had always enjoyed her Monday afternoons,
walking around the market chatting to stallholders,
gathering in the gossip, the gripes, the funny stories.
They were her friends here, as well as her clients. Most
of them had known her father, who had also been the
market PR officer, although the weekly column was
Alice's brain-child.

They were pleased to see her, but right from the
moment she walked in it became one of those days
with more grouses than smiles. She had written two
columns for the weeks she was on holiday, leaving
them at the newspaper office, and there were complaints about both.

The engagement of a couple—who had been starry-
eyed when they told her about it—had ended before
it was announced. Happy Harry, whose patter from
his fruit and veg stall could have the customers roaring

with laughter, and who always had a good story to tell her, had run his van into the back of a steamroller while she was away. Next day, when she had featured him as the merry life and soul of the market hall, he was lying in hospital with a broken leg and a king-size chip on his shoulder.

It seemed to take longer than usual this afternoon, as though everybody had to be placated, either because trade wasn't so good, or because she was just back from a fortnight in Florida and they were fed up. 'All right for some,' she heard again and again. And, 'You're as pasty-faced as when you went; the sun was wasted on you.'

She walked away from them quite glad that her working day was over, hoping that the evening with Martin would be hassle free.

By late afternoon the breeze had developed into a bitter wind, and she was shivering with cold when she got home.

At least there was no sign of the upstairs lodger, and that was a relief. She was over the idiotic notion that he could have been the intruder, but she wanted her home to herself for the rest of this day.

She took her time bathing and changing. Martin was picking her up at seven. They had made no plans, and they would probably end up in his flat, which was self-contained and well equipped.

Alice had spent a lot of time there in recent months, but it was essentially a bachelor pad and she never felt inclined to play the housewife. She cooked sometimes, and often brought food, but she did no tidying up and she took no washing or mending away. Thinking about that, she wondered why Martin and his family thought she was marriage material. She knew she was not, but she did like Martin very much and they got along together very well.

She dressed for herself, she supposed, to please herself, but tonight she chose a short black and white dog-tooth check jacket and a matching straight skirt, worn with a white silk shirt, which was one of his favourite outfits. Her hair fell smoothly from a side parting in a deep, soft wave. It was jaw-length, thick and glossy, and she had no real complaints about her face or her figure.

She looked at her reflection in the long bathroom mirror and thought ruefully, I wouldn't make a bad waxwork or a shop window dummy. There's nothing wrong with me, except that I look as if there's no blood in me.

That was when she saw the ladder in her tights and had to go rooting through her undies drawer for another pair. That was one more small irritation, because this was the first time on, but she was ready at seven when Martin rang her front door bell.

She always knew that he would arrive on the dot, and she could always rely on him for a compliment. 'Evening, darling; you look terrific,' he said, standing there beaming at her.

'Thank you,' she always said, adding, 'So do you,' because, even with his nose skinning, he was impeccably turned out.

You'd make a good tailor's dummy too, she thought, and was ashamed of herself, and drew him into the hall and kissed him warmly to make up for it.

He was a good kisser. His arms held her with just the right pressure and his lips against hers stirred little warm, pleasurable thrills. Over his shoulder she was looking up the stairs at the closed door at the top, and although she knew there was no one there—there wasn't a light showing—she had the feeling that Ivan Blackmore could walk out any moment.

Even if he did, she had a perfect right to make mad, passionate love on her own hall floor if she wanted to, let alone kiss her steady date. But somehow her kissing mood had passed, and that was all Martin had expected anyhow.

When she asked, 'Are we eating at your flat? I bought food this afternoon; shall I bring it along?' he said,

'Good idea,' and let her go.

In the car she told him that Miss Pringle had gone and left a six-month tenant behind. 'His name's Ivan Blackmore; he's a writer.'

'I think I've heard of him,' said Martin. 'Have you met him?'

'Yes.'

'What's he like?'

She thought about that before answering. 'Successful, they say, sure of himself.'

'Young?'

'Youngish—thirtyish.'

'Married?'

'I don't know. There could be a wife joining him; he's on his own now.' It was not a family apartment, with just one large bedroom, but she was almost sure Ivan Blackmore was a lone wolf, a lone tiger.

'If he's living in your house,' said Martin, smiling at her as they stopped at a traffic light, 'I'd be happier if he were happily married.'

Martin was flattered but uneasy that other men fancied Alice. He enjoyed knowing heads turned when

SHADOW OF A TIGER

she was with him and eyes followed her. And at parties
when men vied for her attention he would have liked
to be possessive, but he knew that wouldn't go down
too well with her, so he always tried to joke about it,
although he was not amused.

When she smiled it reassured him.

She didn't smile now. She said, 'Could be; I really
don't know much about him,' and he hoped that
meant she was not interested.

It was almost a hassle-free evening, like so many
that had gone before. She and Martin never rowed.
In the flat he turned on music and set the lights at a
not too bright level. And Alice laid the table and put
out a cold buffet. They sat facing each other, their
plates filled, and talked about the holiday.

Alice said it had been lovely, she had enjoyed it so
much. And Martin said how well she had got on with
his family. Alice said who wouldn't? They were super.
And Martin said his mother had taken to Alice and
was sure they were right for each other.

'She thinks it's time we were settling down, and she's
never wrong, is Mother,' Martin said complacently.
He and his mother certainly believed that, so it seemed
that Alice's protest against getting married hadn't
registered with him. But she couldn't start arguing,
not now.

'Try this pâté,' she said. 'It's a new one. The little
black bits are supposed to be truffles.'

She was usually comfortable with Martin, but
tonight she seemed beset by prickly vibes, as though
the irritations of the afternoon were clinging to her.

After the meal, when they sat on the big, soft sofa
and he tried to make love to her, she said, 'Oh lord,

I'm sorry,' because it was not going to work. She was a long way from melting into his arms.

She felt rigidly unresponsive, which was not all Martin's fault, although when he said, 'This is nothing to do with this man Blackmore, I suppose?' she snapped,

'Don't be stupid,' and said, 'Sorry, sorry,' again. 'I seem to be on a short fuse, but it has been one of those days, and I shouldn't have come out tonight; I'm rotten company. I should have had an early night and woken up a bit less peevish in the morning.'

He was looking understanding—he always did—and she stroked his face. 'I'm a pig to you sometimes, aren't I? I don't know why you put up with me. Why don't you find yourself a nice, reasonable girl?'

'I must like unreasonable women,' he said, and she found herself ruffling his hair as if he were very young, although he was nearly ten years older than she was.

She yawned. 'Would you mind very much if I did go? I've got to be up bright and early for that shop opening in the precinct.'

She knew he wouldn't try to persuade her to stay; Martin never risked a rebuff. Nor was he going to say, 'Then call yourself a cab,' because he was too much of a gentleman.

He drove her home, suffering in silence, and she tried to talk, but couldn't think of much to say, and when they drew up in front of her house he said, 'I always knew you were safe with Miss Pringle upstairs.'

He probably wasn't remembering the break-in. Almost everybody had forgotten that by now. He hadn't known Alice then and they had never discussed it.

'What do you mean, "safe"?' she asked.

'Another woman in the house. I hope this man won't try anything on.'

'If he does,' she said gaily, 'I'll let you know, and you can come and throw him out for me.'

She leaned across and kissed his cheek and was out of the car before he was. He closed his half-open door and waved to her as he drove away. Waving back from the pavement, she thought wryly, A fat lot of use you'd be. Because Martin was one of the nicest of men, but she couldn't imagine him carrying much clout as a protector.

She was a wretch; Martin was too good for her, and now she would call it a day and hope for a brighter tomorrow. She listened to a call from a girlfriend on the answerphone, then went into the kitchen and switched on the kettle, and tuned the radio to the local station.

When the phone rang she collected it from the office and carried it back to the kitchen, spelling out her number. 'Alice?' said a high, shrill voice. 'It's Patsy here. We've got a problem, Alice; Selena can't make it tomorrow.'

'Why not?' She switched off the radio and bit her lip hard, listening to Patsy's hysterical explanation. Then she said, 'All right. Calm down. Don't worry. I'll find you another celebrity before ten o'clock.'

Somebody on her books would surely come along for the publicity of a photograph in the local that was promised, but Patsy was babbling eagerly, 'But you've got a celebrity, haven't you? Somebody told us who he was who's taken over your top floor. Couldn't you ask him?'

'No, I could not,' Alice snapped. 'Leave it with me. I'll start phoning. Get off the line, and I'll ring you back as soon as I've fixed it.'

'But couldn't you at least ask him?' Patsy wailed, and Alice shrieked,

'Not a chance.' This was the last straw. She put down the phone and went on shrieking at it, 'This is all I need to round off today.'

She could have banged the phone against the wall, and she came out of the kitchen screaming silently, then her jaw dropped when she saw Ivan Blackmore halfway down the stairs.

'Ghosts in the kitchen too?' he enquired pleasantly.

'Why can't you stay in your own apartment?' He must be convinced now that she was barking mad, and she waved the phone. 'The hula dancer was on the line. Our local beauty queen should have been opening her shop tomorrow, and now she's out of circulation, and Patsy has heard that the well known writer Ivan Blackmore is on the loose in these parts and wonders if he would mind declaring On the Wild Side open to the public in the morning.'

Now it was his turn to look appalled. 'You are joking?'

'I'm not laughing, but I am joking.' He had stayed where he was, four steps up, and she leaned against the wall, drooping disconsolately. 'Oh, and I'd like my front door key back, please. You shouldn't have it.'

'There's no right of way,' he said before she could. 'Right.'

'Catch.' He dug into his pocket and tossed it down, and of course she missed it. 'What happened to the beauty queen?'

'She's got a black eye.'

'Careless. Although I should have thought a beauty queen would have learned how to blot out a blemish.'

'This is a shiner, and it was careless. She let two boyfriends meet, there was a scuffle, and Selena went out for the count.'

He started to laugh and after a moment so did she. It was a nuisance, and it wasn't that funny, but once she started she found herself pealing with laughter.

'Stand-in for a beauty queen with a black eye,' he said. 'Why not? I've got nothing else on in the morning. All right, I'll do it.'

'You will?' She couldn't believe her luck. 'That would be splendid.' That was nice of him, because he wasn't needing a mention in the local Press, and Patsy's merchandise was not his line of country either. 'You can have the front door key back,' she said, 'and feel free to stroll around the garden any time.'

She picked up the key and offered it to him, and this time when their hands brushed of course she didn't flinch. 'Thank you,' he said.

'Have a good day?' she enquired. 'What was left of it?'

'Yes, how about you?'

She nearly said, Fine, automatically. Instead she admitted, 'Awful. Well, no, not awful, but not one of my best.'

'I'd like to hear about it.'

He had come down the stairs to take the key, so that he was close now, looking down at her from his considerable height, although she was a tall girl, and she was aware of his sensuality like a male aura. But she managed to say lightly enough, 'I don't suppose you would; there wasn't much drama, but it seemed like one damn thing after another.'

'Come up and have a drink?' he suggested.

'You didn't even have coffee this morning; what have you got now?'

'Coffee, a good red wine. I'm stocking up on essentials.'

She was grateful to him for stepping in at short notice, and Patsy would be thrilled. She said, 'Let me phone Patsy, and I'll take you up on the good red.'

Patsy *was* thrilled. She had notices up around town, and she and her staff would be out early to plaster 'Ivan Blackmore, author' over 'Selena Smith, beauty queen'. Alice said she would get the message on local breakfast radio, and Patsy began gleefully rehearsing what she would say to Selena, who had really let her down.

'I thought you were mad about it too,' said Patsy. 'You don't often lose your cool, but I thought you had.'

'Well, let's hope we've got everything under control now,' said Alice.

She took off her jacket and ran a comb through her hair, pushing the heavy waves out of her eyes. Then she went up to the first floor. She had run up these stairs countless times. The carpet was the old dark red patterned Wilton it always had been, but beyond the door at the top were Eleanor Pringle's carpets and pictures and furniture. Alice had become so used to them that they had almost blotted the upstairs landing as it used to be from her mind.

The living-room door was open, and the kitchen door, and he called from the kitchen, 'Go on in.'

Every trace of her old bedroom had vanished, except for the shape of the window. For the last three years this had been a comfortable and charming sitting-room, with easy-chairs, a big faded Chinese carpet and furniture that included several genuine Georgian pieces.

Eleanor would have taken her personal belongings, of course, but she seemed to have left everything else for the tenant's use. The bow-fronted desk had a manual typewriter and a pile of papers on it, and Alice might have crossed to that and taken a quick look if he had not come into the room then with the opened bottle, asking, 'Do you know where the glasses are?'

'Over here.' She opened a low corner cupboard and knelt down in front. Nothing had gone. The glasses were in their matching sets, and she was sorry to think she might never sip a glass with Eleanor Pringle again. They had shared jokes and quiet moments, and it was over.

Unless Eleanor came back. Sometimes people did. At the window he had said, 'I'll be back.' The voice had been low, hoarse... And back for what, for God's sake?

Still on her knees when Blackmore touched her shoulder, she stiffened and said jerkily, 'Some of them are quite valuable. You will be careful with them, won't you?'

She was holding one, and perhaps her hand was not too steady, because he said, 'I won't break them if you don't.'

After that she scrambled to her feet and put two glasses on the small, black-lacquered Chinese tray on the rosewood side-table, and sat down.

She felt more at home in here than she did in Martin's flat. She had washed these wine glasses, vacuumed the carpets, dusted and polished the furniture. Eleanor Pringle did her own housework, but she was no longer young, and Alice had often given a hand, so that this apartment had become almost a second home to her.

She usually sat on a tapestry-covered footstool, but this was when a woman who had been like a kindly aunt was seated in the wing chair. Tonight Alice chose one of the armchairs. Sitting at Ivan Blackmore's feet would have been altogether too twee.

She took the glass he offered her and thanked him and sipped appreciatively, and knew that it was a good wine, less because she was a connoisseur than because she was pretty sure he was.

He sat in an armchair too, leaving Eleanor Pringle's wing chair empty, and, looking at the empty chair, Alice heard herself sigh heavily. 'Miss Pringle's chair?' he said.

'How did you . . . ?' she began. But he had met the retired, upright schoolmarm, and that looked like her kind of chair. And Alice had rushed up to see her last night, so she must be fond of her. It wouldn't be hard to guess why she was sighing. 'Miss Pringle's chair,' she said. 'I can't get over coming back and not finding her. I was so used to having her up here.'

'You don't like change?'

'Sometimes.' New ideas, new projects, were the life-blood of her livelihood, but this was a change she was less happy about.

'I hope you'll get used to this one,' he said, 'but I can't offer to be a stand-in for Miss Pringle.'

'As well as the beauty queen.' A smile tugged the corners of her mouth. 'You don't have much in common with either of them.' You are tougher than both of them put together, for starters... Her smile widened as she went on, 'Miss Pringle is older and Selena's prettier. To be honest, they're both prettier.'

He grinned. 'But I don't have the black eye.'

'Selena will still be gorgeous. Careless but gorgeous.'

The wine was pleasant, and suddenly it seemed a pleasant thing to be sitting here, talking nonsense with this man who had scared her silly—and silly was the word—last night. Changes happened, and she had to accept this one. She asked, 'Are you going to be living here alone?'

'Are you interested?' He held the fragile glass in hands that were strong and steady. Over it he smiled at her, a slightly crooked smile, and they were fencing again, but this time it was a friendly fooling.

She found herself sinking into the armchair, almost kicking off her shoes, and tucking her feet under. Relaxing anyway, telling him, 'Only as a neighbour,' she sipped her drink and said airily, 'But I have a very good friend who is very interested. He would prefer a man with a wife up here. He felt I was safely chaperoned with Miss Pringle.'

'From what I saw of Miss Pringle, you could have been.' She nodded and waited. 'Nobody else is moving in,' he said, and she wondered why she had guessed that when he was so stunningly attractive. Because he was, now she was over her crazy prejudice and ready to accept him as she found him.

The wine had nothing to do with it. She had drunk mineral water with her meal and only taken a few sips

from this glass, but Ivan Blackmore was a danger-
ously sexy man in a maverick fashion. 'And you have
a very good friend,' he said.

'Yes.' She had just told him that. For Alice there
had always been a repeating pattern of doting men,
who often stayed her friends after the affairs ended,
although the one before Martin had gone into a sulk
that still had him crossing roads to avoid speaking to
her.

'Of course,' he said, and as she met his eyes there
was a tingle in the air like a charge of electricity, which
made her blink when she breathed. 'Were you with
him in Florida?'

'Yes.'

'And . . . ?'

'It was lovely. Lovely villa, lovely weather.'

'While you kept out of the sun because you burn.'
She laughed. 'Oh, I got around, under a big hat.'

'Does your very good friend burn?'

'Not at all.' She was not going to say, He turns
pink.

Anyhow, Martin did look fitter for his holiday, but
not with anything like this man's animal vitality. She
could imagine him beneath a blazing sun, muscles
smooth and skin gleaming.

'So what happened today that was one damned
thing after another?' he asked.

Now it was not irritating her any more, she could
see the funny side. She said, 'Right, set the scene: the
market hall. I walk in, all bright-eyed and nice-to-see-
you-again, and every client has a gripe, every blessed
one.'

She described them for him and did the voices,
building up one after another like a comic act, be-

cause he was a smashing listener. When he laughed
with her it was as though they were walking round
together, sharing the jokes as they came.

'Then home,' she said. 'All dressed up, ready to go,
and there's a great ladder in my tights, which is a
flaming nuisance to any woman.'

Some time she had slipped off her shoes, and now
she stretched a long, slim leg and sighed theatrically.
'But as a mere man you can't appreciate that.'

'Believe me, I appreciate it,' he said. She did have
good legs, and she was flirting. So was he, and it was
harmless fun. 'So where did you go, all dressed up?'
he asked.

'Where did *you* go?' She had been doing the talking.
'I've reached seven o'clock tonight. What did you do
after I left you finishing your coffee?'

He had gone walking, following a route she had
told him about over lunch, across the hills, through
a little wood of spruce trees and silver birch, past old
mine workings and what had once been a toll-house.

He hadn't found the toll-house, and when he asked,
'Will you show me where it is?' she said,

'If you like; I often walk up there.'

'On your own?'

She did walk alone. She cleared her head that way.
'Sometimes,' she said.

'Sometimes with this good friend of yours—what's
his name?'

'Martin. What's your best friend called?'

'Do you mean friend or lover? It doesn't always
follow.'

It had with her, but she said, 'Your lover, then—
your partner.'

'My ex answers to Felicity.'

'Ex-wife?'

'No.'

'Ever been married?'

'No.'

'Ever wanted to be?'

'Never.'

Talking was unhurried and easy. She was curled into the deep chair now, and he sat opposite, the long, strong body relaxed, a man who was right out of the usual run and who fancied her. She knew that as surely as she knew that she was beginning to fancy him.

'Me neither,' she said, 'but it's a problem that crops up.'

'I can see how it might.' The look he gave her now was open admiration, and the warmth of the room was bringing colour to her face. Or perhaps it was the wine. 'You're star quality,' he said. 'You'd easily upstage most women.'

That was going over the top—he was probably fooling a little there—and she said, 'I don't know about that, but you must have come across a few wannabee wives in your time. You're eligible—you could be notorious for all I know; I haven't read the book yet—and successful.'

'Solvent at any rate.'

'That's high on many a woman's list,' she joked.

'Not on yours?'

'Of course on mine. Solvency's there all right, but marriage isn't.'

They were both smiling, and if he had reached across and taken her hand she would have let his fingers clasp hers.

'It doesn't figure on my list either.' His voice was a lazy drawl. 'We could have something going here.'

With a man like him you would know exactly where you stood. He wouldn't be laying claim to body and soul.

'Grounds for discussion?' she said lightly.

'Definitely.'

The grandfather clock in the hall below struck the hour, and this time she counted and it was late. 'I must go,' she said.

He got up when she did. 'What time in the morning?' he asked.

'I'll see you around nine-thirty. Is that OK?'

'I'll be with you.'

They walked to the door at the top of the stairs and she said, 'Thanks for tomorrow, and for the wine.'

'Thank you.'

She nearly said, What for? It was not as if she had done anything or offered anything, but, looking up into his dark eyes with a deep line cutting between them, she could feel his mouth on hers, although he never touched her.

'Goodnight,' he said.

'Goodnight,' she echoed. She went downstairs and heard the door closing above her, and shut the bathroom door behind her and ran cold water into her cupped hands and bathed her face.

Eligible, she had said, attracting women because he was well known and solvent. She could have said that he would have no trouble at all turning on your average woman, because he had the devil's own sensuality. And she looked at her reflection, with the water dripping off her chin, and remembered how she had looked a few hours earlier, waiting for Martin: bored stiff and neat as a shop window dummy.

She was very much alive now, with her hair falling over shining eyes and the two top buttons of her shirt undone—she must have fiddled with them as she talked. The thin silk seemed to cling to the rise and fall of her breasts, and colour came and went in her cheeks.

She had always landed herself with men who became too possessive, and now she had the old trouble again with Martin. It wouldn't happen with Blackmore. He needed his space and he would leave her hers; so he could well be right—there could be something going between them. Something mutually satisfying and undemanding.

She began to undress, but when she had stripped off she caught her reflection again, slender and pale, and she reached hurriedly for her pyjamas, because a memory of being naked and helpless was falling across her like a dark shadow. She almost ran from the bathroom, muffled in her towelling robe, and by the time she was in bed the memory and the shadow were gone.

She was fine. Tomorrow was going to be great. Nothing was happening to her with which she could not cope.

CHAPTER THREE

NEXT morning Alice had second thoughts. Last night she had found the man upstairs sexy and stimulating and apparently feeling the same about her. Last night the idea of an affair between them had seemed very tempting.

It still did, but she was calmer now, warier, and in no rush to fall into the arms of somebody who could walk in on her any hour of the day or night. A lover under the same roof might be too close for comfort, and taking on a man practically on sight would be madly irresponsible.

She had never been that impulsive. She needed more than lust and shared laughter before her link with Ivan Blackmore became passionate and intimate, and she was very glad that she had not ended up in bed with him last night.

She might have done, given a little more time and a little more persuasion—the sexual attraction had been astonishing—and that could have put her at a disadvantage this morning. Instead of which she would get on with today with an untroubled mind.

If he was here for six months she could take a few weeks to decide how far she was going with him, but, in the meantime, knowing he was upstairs now was already giving a buzz to her day.

Half-nine, she had said. It was ten minutes to the hour, and at twenty-five past she would tap on the door at the top of the stairs and hope he was ready.

If he appeared bleary-eyed he would have to move if they were to be at the precinct for ten, but somehow she couldn't imagine him oversleeping. It was hard to imagine him sleeping at all. Even relaxed, as he had been last night in the sitting-room with her, there was still that feeling of latent power about him.

She made her two phone calls: one to the radio station that was broadcasting an ad for this morning's opening of On the Wild Side, to explain that Selena Smith was out and Ivan Blackmore was in; the other to the local paper, making sure their photographer was turning up and telling him who they would be photographing.

The chief photographer wanted to know how she had got hold of Blackmore, and she said gaily, 'Oh, he's living with me,' and as the pressman whistled she laughed and explained, 'He's the tenant in the upstairs flat; I've only just met him.'

In the few minutes she had to spare she took a bottle of Brasso and two dusters outside to rub up the brass plate by the front door. Tarnish had given the metal a pale green sheen, and she was applying the polish vigorously when the postman handed her her mail.

There was only one letter this morning, addressed in Eleanor Pringle's hand and postmarked Bath, and she tore open the envelope to read Eleanor's goodbye. They had managed to get a cancellation for her on a flight, and, by the time this reached Alice, Eleanor's niece and her niece's husband would have waved her off.

It was goodbye, but it was a letter to treasure. She wrote glowingly and gratefully of Alice's thoughtfulness for her.

I know how lucky I have been, finding a girl who was like a daughter—or should I say grand-daughter?—to me. Dear Alice, you were always a joy and I shall miss you so very much...

Alice slipped the letter into her pocket and poured more polish on the cloth and went on rubbing, hearing in her mind Eleanor's words spoken in that clear no-nonsense voice. Miss Pringle had had no time for sen-timentality, but Alice was touched to learn how much she had meant to her old friend.

She would miss Eleanor. She would be a little lonelier for losing her, and sudden tears were misting her eyes, until she dabbed with fingertips along her lashes, blotting them away. Then she went on pol-ishing the plaque, and behind her Ivan Blackmore said, 'Morning.'

She spun round. 'Where have you sprung from?' That was obvious when he was carrying a paper from the newspaper shop. Alice had her morning paper de-livered, but she didn't think she wanted to share it, and it was not the one he had bought...and why was he staring at her?

'Is it intentional, or do you have black eyes too?' he enquired.

Her fingers were tacky, and she must have smudged metal polish on her face. She said, 'I got my hair in my eyes.' She was lucky she hadn't rubbed the polish into her eyes, or it would have been stinging like mad. Now she would have to clean her face as well as wash her hands. Time was getting tight, the brass plate was still smeared, and Martin's car was drawing up in front of the house.

He sometimes came this way to town and his office, but usually he took a shorter route, and if he was curious about the new tenant he couldn't have timed it better. He came down the path to the front door, his eyes fixed on Blackmore, and as he reached them Alice went through the introductions.

'I've heard a lot about you,' Blackmore said amiably. Martin didn't seem too happy about that, and Alice wouldn't have thought she had done that much talking about Martin. But it could be meeting Blackmore, who would rate a second look any time, that was bothering Martin.

'I just dropped in,' he said to Alice, 'to say I'll collect you at seven tonight.'

'No, you won't.' She would almost certainly be busy. 'Sorry, but this evening's out.'

'Tomorrow, then?'

If she had not been running late she would have gone into details, explaining that she hadn't got herself organised yet after her holiday, but it was going to be a rush from here, so she smiled and said briefly, 'I'll phone you.'

'Please do that,' said Martin, understanding as always. 'Or I'll phone you.'

He kissed her cheek, grimacing slightly as he tasted metal polish. As he got into the car Blackmore said, 'There goes an obliging man.'

'We try to oblige each other,' she said sweetly.

'Seemed rather one-sided to me. Pity about his nose. Did the sun catch him?'

'You,' she said, 'have no cause to be critical about noses.' He grinned, and she decided, 'I'll have to finish this when I get back.'

'Give me the rag.'

Her lips parted to warn him, Don't get it on your hands, but she shut her mouth because this man was not for nannying. So she said, 'Thanks,' and hurried into the house. If they walked down they would be cutting it fine, so she would take her car, and, cleaned up, she re-read Eleanor's letter and put it away in her bureau.

The brass plaque was unsmeared and shining when she came out of the garage. After her father's death she had neglected his name-plate for a while. Grief, and struggling to keep a business afloat, and the chaos of conversion so that she could sell upstairs and pay off debts, had filled her mind and her time. But when she had noticed the tarnish on it she had spent hours rubbing away the verdigris and bringing the brightness back.

She liked to see his name there. Her life had been sunny while he lived. He had been a generous, good-humoured man, with a rumbling laugh that she could still hear sometimes when she was alone.

This morning his name shone beautifully. Blackmore was waiting out here, and she said, 'You've made a super job of this; I'd recommend you any time.'

'Nice to know I could get a reference; I've just been asked if I'm an odd-job man.'

'You what?' she yelped. 'Who asked you that?' He was wearing the same grey suit as yesterday, this time with a dark grey sweater. A very expensive suit. Even with a rubbing rag in his hands, nobody could seriously have mistaken him for a casual labourer.

'A woman in a purple tracksuit and pink-framed spectacles. Lives over the road.'

She grinned at that, recognising a neighbour with an eye for the men. Seeing Ivan Blackmore on her morning jog, his height, and the boxer's shoulders under the well cut jacket, would have had her smiling even before he turned round. She wouldn't have been able to resist chatting him up. 'Did she offer you a job?' Alice gurgled.

'It was a near thing.'

'I'll bet it was. She's a well heeled divorcee; you'd have got good terms there.' The curtains would be twitching in the house across the way. 'By the way, you aren't charging for this morning, are you?'

'What was the beauty queen getting?'

A modest fee and the publicity, but Alice said blithely, 'I think she was taking it in scarlet undies.'

'Fascinating.'

He looked at his watch and she said, 'We'll take my car.'

She got it out of the garage, a white Astra with the black question mark logo on the doors, and as he opened the passenger door he said, 'It suits you. Miss Enigma.' His legs were too long, and he fiddled with the mechanism, pushing the seat back to its limit.

'What's puzzling about me?' She moved into the morning traffic, watching the road, but sensing the quizzical look he turned on her. Funny that, the way she could feel him looking at her.

'The contradictions,' he said. 'A cool lady who jumps out of her skin.'

'Only once in a while.' Twice. For a reason she could never explain.

'And this good friend of yours. It's another mystery what you're doing with him.'

'Not to me it isn't.' And she was glad all over again that last night's get-together had ended when it did. This man might not be possessive, but he was aggravating, and it might be smarter to keep their relationship platonic. Friendly, though. For the next few hours she was not riling her star turn.

'What's his line?' he was asking, but she did not want to discuss Martin. He had many good qualities, but none that would impress Ivan Blackmore.

'He's an accountant,' she said shortly.

'Useful.'

'Very. Now let me tell you what the set-up is with the shop.' She could talk herself into town on this, and she launched into an account of the fairground folk who were Patrice Perinni's family.

'When the fair closed down Patsy's grandparents and parents settled here, and the women opened a market stall. Patsy has a flair for design and she specialises in clothes with a Romany touch—originals; they have a workroom and they produce some lovely things.'

She told him about the family and friends and staff he would be meeting. 'Granny Rosa, but I don't think she'll be there. She's a born traveller. She still has her caravan in the grounds of the house and she looks on the last twenty years as a temporary stay. Patsy was in two minds whether to tell her about the shop, and so far she seems to be ignoring it.'

'Why aren't you wearing a Romany special for the grand opening?' he asked her.

She was in a stone-coloured sweater, jacket and skirt, with soft leather brown boots and a shoulder purse, and she shrugged. 'I'm the wrong colouring.'

'You could always settle for the scarlet undies.'

She nearly quipped back, How do you know I haven't? but this morning flirting did not seem quite as harmless as it had last night, so she laughed instead and said, 'She does some brilliant kerchiefs. If you fancy one I'll get it for you.'

'That's generous. You look around and I'll buy you your choice.'

'Don't be hasty,' she joked. 'We could be into designer prices here.'

'All right,' he said, and then she sobered suddenly, because it would be awful if he thought she'd manoeuvred his offer, and she began to stammer,

'I'm joking; I wouldn't——'

'I'm sure you wouldn't,' he said drily. 'There's no need to labour the point.'

She felt deflated and gave all her attention to parking the car in the delivery yard behind the shops. Then she said, 'Ready for the big moment?'

'I think I'll manage to cut the ribbon.'

He was smiling, probably laughing at her calling the opening of a small shop unit a big moment, and she wished that Selena had kept out of harm's way and turned up this morning. Selena would have enjoyed the razzmatazz that would be cheap and tawdry by sophisticated standards.

And Patsy's family and friends were Alice's friends, but Ivan Blackmore would be viewing them cynically, and suddenly she wanted to get him away from them as soon as possible. It would be hurtful and embarrassing if he showed them he was bored.

She said, 'You don't have to hang about. If you just say the shop's open and good luck to everybody you can remember an appointment and go.'

'Why?'

She had switched off the ignition. Now she turned in her seat to face him and said, 'Well, you'd probably be bored if you stayed.' Depression was settling on her; she wouldn't stay long herself.

Then he kissed her, cupping her chin in his hand and bending his head to brush her lips lightly and swiftly, a pressure of a few seconds, but warming her blood like getting a fix of pure joy, so that laughter began to bubble up inside her.

'On the other hand,' she said, 'we could have a ball.'

'I'm banking on it.' He came round the car as she locked her door, and took her hand, and they walked together across the yard, towards the open back door of the shop, where someone was smiling and waving.

Dancers must feel this way she felt when they found the right partner. He was taller than she was, his stride would be longer, but they walked as if they were in tune. And she thought crazily, We fit together; physically we are a perfect match. Just standing close to him could be almost like making love.

Patsy came running out, dark hair braided, her dress a rainbow swirl of colours. Hugging Alice, her eyes all for Ivan, she began thanking them both. 'Everybody's here and waiting; now all we need are you and the customers. Oh, Alice, I hope I'm doing the right thing. I'm so nervous, and guess what—Granny Rosa's turned up. You don't think she's going to put a hex on it, do you?' She explained to Ivan, 'She's my grandmother and she can be a right old witch.'

'I can't wait to meet her,' he said, and Patsy said,

'Everybody's dying to meet you. Thank you ever so much for coming.'

They went through the store-room into the shop, where dark crimson walls and gilded paintwork provided a striking theatrical background for the racks and displays of brightly coloured clothes. Big bunches of balloons and a finger-buffet and soft drinks struck a festive note, with the little gathering inside the shop tensed up like runners waiting for the starter's pistol.

The talking stopped when Alice and Ivan walked in and started again as Patsy began introducing several of them to him. Alice had expected a junior photographer, but Owen French, head of department, ginger-haired and wiry, had turned up himself and was waiting with a wide grin and an outstretched hand.

'Good to meet you again,' said Owen, and Ivan looked pleased to see him, and Alice thought, I must have a word with Owen as soon as I get the chance.

Quite a crowd had gathered in the precinct, peering into the shop over the red ribbon across the open doorway, and out there music was playing. A girl with a tambourine and a young man with a fiddle had been drumming up interest down the high street, and were now doing their turn in front of the shop.

The only unsmiling face was Granny Rosa's. Patsy had found her a chair tucked away at the back of the shop, and there she sat in a black dress and a wealth of gold jewellery, wrinkled and dour, and looking quite capable of casting the evil eye on the proceedings.

Ivan had met her. Patsy had taken him up and a few words were spoken, and when Ivan and Patsy and the Press slipped out of the back door, to walk round to the front of the shop, Alice wondered if she should go up to Patsy's grandmother and plead with her not to spoil Patsy's big day.

Perhaps it was better to leave well alone. She was not family, and her interference might be resented. Besides, there was hardly time. Ivan had made a short speech and 'opened' the shop. The customers were coming in, camera flashlights were popping as Owen French got his pictures, and the cash till was ringing.

Alice circulated and thought how well it was going, with the party spirit everywhere. Owen French had to leave for another assignment, but as he went he called to Ivan, 'I'll see you then.'

'Right,' Ivan called back, so it looked as though they had arranged a meeting, and Alice would have to wait for another opportunity to ask the photographer where he and Ivan Blackmore had met before.

Ivan was talking to Granny Rosa, and Alice was deliberately avoiding looking like a hanger-on by following him around. Besides, she didn't have to. In the small shop she could always hear his voice if she listened for it. She could turn her head and catch his eye, and then his smile would reach her like a secret and intimate touch. Even when he was at the back of the shop, talking to the old gypsy woman, and Alice was trying on a silk jacket just inside the front door, she felt the invisible bond between them as if they were still holding hands.

He was the main attraction here—almost the only male in a shop full of females—and those who didn't know he was a writer thought he had to be an actor, with those looks and that larger-than-life personality.

But another—and more surprising—star was Granny Rosa.

When Ivan spoke to Patsy and she moved a small table forward in front of her grandmother, chewing on an underlip and looking apprehensive, Alice presumed that Granny wanted her cookies and plastic cup of fruit punch served in style.

Granny Rosa was smiling, a close-lipped smile, but an improvement on her scowl. And nothing was being served up to her. She was opening for business, palms read for free on proof of a purchase.

It was a roaring success, and the old fairground kiosk patter tripped off her tongue as if it were two weeks, not two decades, since the Perrini travelling fair had ground to a halt. What was more—to Patsy's relief—she was sending them all away happy.

'Why didn't I think of this?' Patsy asked Alice, and it was a gimmick that had never occurred to Alice, who had thought Granny Rosa was more likely to scupper Patsy's project than help it.

But she seemed to be enjoying herself now that Ivan Blackmore had coaxed her into joining in. 'Good work,' said Alice, nodding towards Granny, who held the hand of a middle-aged housewife and was telling her something that had her giggling. 'How did you do it?'

'I hate to see talent wasted,' he said.

'She must have been a knock-out thirty years ago,' Alice mused softly.

'She still is,' he said, and now she could see for herself the high cheekbones under the brown wrinkled skin, and the dark eyes that were still lustrous.

'Alice?' said Granny.

The other chair was empty for the moment, but Alice held back. She had never cared for the idea of somebody telling *her* something she might not have wished to tell them. Nor did she really want to know what her future held. Sometimes she feared it might be pretty bleak. She said, 'Ivan, why don't you let her read your hand?' and immediately everyone around joined in the chorus.

He sat down and the old woman reached for his left hand. 'Left tells what you were born with,' she informed him, 'your early days. Right tells what you've made of your life. We start with the left.'

Alice found herself leaning across, watching Granny's claw-like forefinger tracing the lines.

'Always had good family, good friends. A good start you had. See, here's the heart line.' Her dark eyes, veiled by papery blue-veined lids, looked down and then flickered up, searching his face for clues, Alice suspected, as much as his hand.

But the patter never faltered. She moved to the right hand and told him he was doing well for himself. 'Always known what you wanted, always got it. Oh, yes,' said Granny Rosa, 'you'll never go short of a bob or two.'

When she finished he held on to her hand and smiled at her. Then he said softly, 'You're an old con merchant,' and Alice thought, She'll go spare; because, as long as she could remember Granny Rosa's firecracker temper had kept her family on the hop.

But she gave a surprisingly girlish toss of the head. 'Takes one to know one,' said Granny and chuckled. Then she turned to grab Alice's arm and said, 'No.'

'No, what?' asked Alice.

'Not for you, young Alice. This is a dangerous man.'

'Aren't they all?' Alice said lightly, and maybe Granny was just getting some drama into her act, but the bony fingers tightened on her arm and she was glad that a girl was saying,

'Me next,' and wriggling into the chair Ivan had just vacated, because something that could have been pity flickered in the old dark eyes, and whether Alice was imagining that or not it still sent a shiver down her spine.

Before she went home Alice slipped across to the delicatessen to buy croissants, and on her way back, just outside the shop, she came face to face with Robin Hailey. That happened occasionally; they both lived and worked in this small town, but both avoided confrontations if they could.

Robin had fallen hard for Alice almost twelve months ago and had taken her drawing back from total commitment badly. Although he had always known she meant to stay single, whenever they did cross each other's paths he always managed to make her feel that she had kicked a friendly dog.

Today there was no dodging. They were within touching distance before they knew it, and Alice said, 'Hello.'

Robin stared at her with mournful eyes. Then he said, 'Still as beautiful as ever,' and sighed.

'Why, thank you; everything all right?' Alice asked idiotically, and got a bitter laugh.

As it happened, she had heard that Robin was dating a girl who worked for the firm he worked for, but he was still wearing his heart on his sleeve for the one that got away, and Alice got away again, trying to smile and mumbling something about it being all go.

In the shop she bought a green silk scarf, and tried on the embroidered jacket once more, and when Ivan tapped his watch and raised an eyebrow she nodded, ready to go and reading the signal. They could leave now; they had more than done their bit for Patsy.

Patsy kissed Alice goodbye, untied one of the few balloons that had not been handed out to the children, and wound the string round Alice's wrist and joked, 'You must take something home from the party.'

She thanked Ivan again. She didn't kiss him goodbye, although she would have liked to very much, and she watched him leave with Alice and thought that some girls seemed to be born lucky.

Outside, after the warmth and bustle in the shop, it seemed cold to Alice. The breeze was skittish, and as she turned the key in her car door the string of the balloon slid from her wrist, and it went up and off on a gust of wind.

She watched it go and said, 'I've always wanted to go up in a balloon.'

'What's stopping you?'

'I don't know.' There were lots of things she wanted to do, some time.

She got into the car and opened the passenger door for him, and as she drove out of the yard he asked, 'What had you done to that poor devil you met in the precinct?'

The shock of that took her breath away, but she managed to say coldly, 'You don't miss much, do you?'

'Not much.'

She was not going to be cross-examined. She snapped, 'We had a disagreement,' and turned on the radio, with the volume high enough to drown any further conversation. She sometimes felt guilty about Robin, and she was damned if she was discussing him with a stranger. So far as she was concerned the

subject was closed, and she kept her mouth shut tight
for the few minutes it took to drive home and into
the garage.

When she switched off the radio he said, 'And I
thought ghetto-blasters were going out of fashion.' She
ignored that, opening the connecting door to the house
and hurrying to answer the phone that was ringing in
the office.

It was Martin, who had phoned before, he said,
and she explained, 'I stayed on for a while in the shop.
It went very well.'

'Well, you're back now, so it's all right for tonight,
is it?'

'No, I told you no.'

'I've got a surprise for you,' said Martin.

'Have you?'

'Can you guess?'

'I'm not very good at guessing.'

'Something to help you change your mind,' said
Martin, and she was almost certain it was a ring and
that this was going to end in a painful scene.

But over the phone, with Ivan Blackmore just
outside the door, she could only delay matters, and
she said, 'Look, I've just got in; I'm busy right now.'

'How about later?' said Martin, and she said
wearily,

'I told you, I'll phone you. Just leave it at that,
will you?' and put down the phone.

'Martin?' said the man in the doorway.

'Yes.' It was a high doorway, wide, but he seemed
to fill it, standing there, looking at her, asking her,
'Do you always choose wimps?'

For a few seconds she blinked, wondering what he
was talking about. But Ivan Blackmore had hit on the

truth. The men in her love-life had been intelligent and understanding, but there hadn't been a strong man among them, and she didn't bother to deny it. She said, 'I don't like being pushed around.'

'You seem to do the shoving.'

'Yes, well,' she said, 'I had a very forceful father. He brought me up single-handed, and what he said went.'

That was not true. Her father had never said no to her in his life. But it was the kind of explanation people expected. 'Since I've been on my own,' she elaborated, 'I've kept clear of dominating men. Any objections? Not that it's any of your business.'

'None at all,' he agreed cheerfully, 'except I'm beginning to feel sorry for them. Martin seems set for the chop, and the bloke in the precinct looked as if you'd left a knife between his shoulderblades when you walked away smiling.'

She had not really been smiling, but Robin had probably stared after her with that wounded look, and what was she supposed to do about it?

She went towards the door into her bed-sit—she wasn't edging past him to get into the hall—but before she reached it he said, 'You're beautiful enough to almost get away with murder,' and she turned again to face him.

'So long as you stay with the wimps,' he said. 'But watch out that one of the other sort never gets you in his sights.'

He looked at her with the steady, unblinking eyes of a hunter, and she found herself backing as he smiled down into her suddenly frightened face.

CHAPTER FOUR

ALICE closed the dividing door between the two rooms behind her, then leant back against it for a moment, breathing hard and telling herself to calm down because there was no reason at all to feel threatened.

Of course she was not being hounded. Words she could deal with. He could say what he liked, the man with the lazy grin that didn't always reach his eyes. She could give as good as she got with words, and at any sign of physical harassment she would put up the barriers so fast...

No man was mastering her. Nobody had since that dreadful night. Compared to Ivan Blackmore, the men she had chosen so far had been wimps, but he could have no idea how fiercely determined she was to take control of her own life.

She could afford to smile. She was in no danger, but this clash of temperaments was striking some lively sparks. Up to a point, she thought, she would enjoy playing the game of seeing how far she could safely go.

The predictability of Martin and those who had gone before had bored her in the end, but Ivan Blackmore was a complex and surprising man, and a challenge she could not resist.

She went back into her office. The room was empty, the door into the hall was closed, and she took out a file she would be working on for the next few days— the marketing plan for a new interior design business that a couple were starting. Alice was the consultant, and she had ideas.

Not long afterwards she heard the front door close and, without lifting her head, which was bowed over papers on her desk, she watched him walk down the road.

When he was out of sight she could still see him in her mind's eye and she wondered where he was going, faintly puzzled, as if she had expected him to look in and tell her. Although why should he?

He hadn't looked towards the window, where she was squinting up through her long lashes. He had not been thinking of her, but she was very aware of him, and that was a new experience for her. She was sensitive and receptive. She had good friends to prove it. But she had never met a man before whom she couldn't get out of her mind.

Even at her busiest she had heard the quiet closing of the front door, and watched to see him pass the window. And now she could imagine him walking away down the road as clearly as if she had opened the window and leaned out.

She brought his book out again and opened it to the photograph inside the back cover. The face seemed as familiar to her as if she had known him for years, and she knew the shape of his hands, the feel of his long body beside her in the car, fingers lifting her chin and a mouth brushing hers with a swift sensuousness that sent happiness surging through her.

She smiled again now, stroking the line of hair as Granny Rosa's forefinger had traced his palm, and told the photograph, 'You're not the most gorgeous hunk I have ever met, but you could be the toughest, so I had better watch that I don't get obsessive about you.'

The ring of the doorbell startled her. As it went on ringing she shut the book and went to answer it, brisk and businesslike, and looking much too level-headed to be wasting her time chatting up a photograph.

'Hello there,' said the woman with her finger on the bell. She had changed out of her purple tracksuit into a lilac polka-dot dress and jacket, but she still wore the pink-rimmed spectacles, and behind the glasses her eyes shone.

'Hello,' said Alice.

Karen Morton and Alice Ashby were neighbours who greeted each other when they met around town, and knew what they heard about each other from mutual acquaintances. Karen was a comparative new-comer, buying her house two years ago after a divorce and a generous settlement. She had joined the singles club, a sports club and the local dramatics society, but Alice belonged to none of these, although the gossip had reached her that Karen made a beeline for the men wherever she went, and most of the women thought she was a pain.

But she was pretty, not all that much older than Alice, rounded and dimpled, and the big spectacles gave her a little-girl-lost look. It hadn't surprised Alice that she had asked Ivan if he was helping out over here; she was always knocking on doors and asking if the man of the house would come and catch a mouse or fix a fuse. Wives and girlfriends had started sug-gesting she look up professional help in the Yellow Pages, and this was the first time she had called on Alice.

She wouldn't be wanting a public relations service; she had to be after Ivan, and she hadn't a hope. Alice could have told her that without bothering to let her in, but of course she had to say, 'Do come in,' and Karen followed her into the office.

'All on your own?' Karen enquired.

'Yes. What can I do for you?'

'I saw him go out,' said Karen. 'I met him this morning; did he tell you?'

'He mentioned it.'

'Who *is* he?' She sounded as excited as a talent scout spotting an undiscovered mega-star, and Alice could understand that someone like Ivan Blackmore would have this effect on someone like Karen Morton. Hard luck for Karen that he was not undiscovered.

'Didn't he tell you who he is?' she said.

'No.' Karen made her eyes even larger. 'I introduced myself and made a little joke about him being an odd-job man, and he laughed.'

'Very witty,' Alice said drily, and as Karen waited expectantly she said, 'His name's Ivan Blackmore and he's moved into what was Miss Pringle's apartment.'

The name was in bold black lettering on the front of the book, and Karen's gaze fixed on it. 'Yes,' Alice said, 'that's the one.'

'Aha.' Karen picked up the book. She opened it and saw the library sticker, turned the page to the 'By the Same Author' list, and said, 'You got this out of the library, did you? Oh, I love his books; I've read all of them. I've got to meet him.'

Not before you've read at least one of them, Alice thought cynically, and was sure that Karen would be shopping for paperbacks this afternoon. She said,

'He's working on a book at the moment; he won't be doing much socialising.'

Karen was trying to work out the set-up. She knew that Miss Pringle's apartment had been up for sale, and now this dishy man had arrived, living in the same house as Alice Ashby. But Alice had a steady; she'd just come back from a holiday in Florida with him. 'Do you know him well?' Karen demanded.

'Very well indeed,' Alice said emphatically, and although Karen was used to women looking daggers at her, accepting it as a tribute to her man appeal, Alice's cool scrutiny shut her up for a moment.

Then she said, 'Well, I'm thrilled—one of my favourite authors moving into our road.'

'Which is your favourite book?' Alice enquired sweetly, and was amused to see Karen floundering, pretending to consider, then bluffing, 'I've enjoyed them all; I don't think I have a favourite.'

'I liked *A Circle of Strangers*,' said Alice, and Karen nodded.

'Oh, so did I.'

Did you? thought Alice, who had just made that title up, confirming her suspicion that Karen was only a fan because he was tall, dark and sexy, and that she probably hadn't read a word he'd written.

Neither had Alice, but she had admitted it, and Karen was starting to irritate her.

'Would you like to come over for dinner some time, or just for a drink?' said Karen, who had never issued any invitations before, and Alice said,

'Do you mean just me?' and had Karen stuttering in her haste to stress that she meant both of them.

What she did mean, of course, was just Ivan, but at first she was prepared to include Alice, who said solemnly, 'That is kind of you,' knowing that kindness had nothing to do with it.

After Karen's visit she felt she could understand the women who had told her, from time to time, that Karen Morton was a menace. Hardly in this case, though. Alice was sure that she was not Ivan Blackmore's type. He might be a womaniser. He had charmed a few over the past few days. And it wasn't true Alice knew him very well, but surely he wouldn't be interested in someone as shallow and silly as Karen?

She made herself a cup of coffee and took it to her desk, picking up the little paper bag containing the sweater scarf she had bought from Patsy's. It was a lovely colour, the bright green of wet grass, and she tucked it into the neck of her sweater while she went on with the dossier she was preparing.

A husband and wife team were setting up on their own, using their home as a showplace for reasonably priced décor and furnishings, aiming at a young clientele rather than the well heeled. She had just finished what would be a magazine features article and sat back, flexing her shoulder muscles, when Ivan walked in.

This time she hadn't heard him coming, but she found that she was pleased to see him. She said, 'You've missed the lady who's looking for an odd-job man. She's thought of something she needs fixing and she left an invitation for you, starting with dinner or drinks. I told her I was sure you'd be right over.'

'Did you, now?' His expression left no doubt what he thought about that, and she grinned.

'Well, no, I didn't. After Granny Rosa's warning, I didn't think it was fair to encourage her. If you're too dangerous for me you're too dangerous for her.'

'That's logical.' He sat on the side of the desk. 'I like your scarf.'

'I got it from Patsy's.' He had probably seen her buying it. 'I liked the colour. I told you to choose one. You can have this if you like.'

She took it off and handed it to him. It made him look like a gypsy or a pirate and for a moment it gave her a jolt, like glimpsing another facet of his character, although she said lightly, 'It suits you.'

'It suits you better.' He untied it and leaned over to fasten it round her throat again, his fingers hardly brushed her skin, but she felt it like a light electric shock. 'Can you spare five minutes?' he said. 'I want to show you something.'

She nearly rubbed her neck where the tingle had been, but twisted her fingers together instead and asked, 'What?'

'Come and see.'

She followed him upstairs. On the old Chinese carpet was a scarlet carrier bag with 'On the Wild Side' in flowing gold lettering, and on Miss Pringle's wing chair was a padded silk jacket. It was the one she had fancied herself in—oyster-grey silk with a sinuous stretching cat appliquéd on the back.

'Who's this for?' she asked.

'You, of course.'

'I hope you got it on approval.'

'Don't you like it?'

He had seen her preening herself in front of the mirror in it, but she said, 'I can't take this.'

'Why not?'

'Well, it's pricey.' Although none of Patsy's stuff was lunatically priced. 'And I don't take ...'

She hesitated, and he suggested, 'Sweets from strangers?' He was laughing at her, but she knew what she meant.

'So it sounds stupid,' she conceded, 'but I don't like feeling in debt.'

She was only just squaring the accounts her open-handed father had left. Paying her way was second nature to her now. Even on holiday with Martin's family she had always come back from shops and markets loaded with food and bottles.

He picked up the coat and looked from it to her, an eyebrow raised. 'What do you think I'd consider myself owed for this?'

And she quoted wryly, '"Ay, there's the rub".'

'You certainly have some complexes: marriage, macho men, freebies.'

'Now where did I hear there's no such thing as a free freebie?' She was making a fuss and making a mess of it, but she looked at him steadily. 'So what would you be expecting in return?'

He looked steadily back. 'You undervalue yourself,' he said, and he dropped the coat on the chair again. 'Or overvalue this. A thank-you would settle it. A smile might be going over the top.'

Of course it wouldn't put her in his debt. He wasn't showering her with diamonds. There was no need to be so stuffy over a friendly gesture, and her smile was shamefaced. 'Well. All right, thank you; it's lovely.' She held out her hands and he put the jacket into them. 'I love the cat,' she said, holding it up to admire Patsy's design of a languorous Siamese.

'Nothing more enigmatic than a cat.' He had called her Miss Enigma. 'And she's got your colouring,' he said. The cat was done in silk of pale caramel, the colour of Alice's hair, but Alice's eyes were grey, not bright blue.

'Not my eyes,' she said. 'But how about the claws?'

'No doubt about the claws.'

They laughed together and she asked, 'Did you eat at the buffet?'

'No.'

'Neither did I. I'm going to make myself a sandwich or something; will you join me?'

'Of course.'

She teased, 'Or you could nip over the road and see if Karen has a better offer.'

'Karen, is it? No, thanks.'

'I did tell her you were working on a book and wouldn't be doing much gadding about.'

'Thank you.'

No trouble at all, she thought; I enjoyed doing it. But she mustn't make a habit of keeping women away from him. It was none of her business whom he got to know while he was here, nor how well.

In the kitchen she buttered the croissants and took down a jar of strawberry preserve, produced a cut loaf, ham, pickles and cheese, and made sandwiches while the kettle boiled for instant coffee.

It was a small kitchen, with a table and four chairs in the same light oak as the Welsh dresser. When she had guests for meals she opened a gate-leg table in her living-room, and she might have carried the tray through there, but he was examining the mugs on the dresser, so she sat down at the kitchen table.

'They're not worth much,' she said. 'I haven't got any rare old pieces. I bought the first years ago because it was cheap and pretty, and suddenly I was into a collection. They're mostly junk, but I like them.'

One of her favourites was the one she was using now, with the little gold hearts and the daisy chains. She held that in both hands and looked at it fondly, and he said, 'You like your possessions around you, don't you?'

'Yes, I do.' There was nothing wrong with that. Most of the furniture had been here in her parents' days. Some she had bought for herself, but everything was here because she liked it. She asked, 'How about you? Miss Pringle has very good furniture, but it isn't yours. Do you mind that?'

'Not at all.'

'Do you collect anything?'

'No.'

She wondered what the house in Cornwall was like, but it was not easy to fit him into a background. Just now, in the green scarf, he had looked like a gypsy. Upstairs among Miss Pringle's Georgian pieces she could imagine him in the boots, breeches, jacket and cravat of a Regency buck.

'Where did they come from?' he asked.

'What? Oh, the mugs.' None of them had been a brilliant find, but the daisy mug was Victorian, and she had found that in a Brighton bygones shop one hot summer's day. Others were from jumble sales, street markets; some were gifts. She could remember how she came by all of them, and she told the tales of a few, while they ate sandwiches and drank coffee.

When the phone rang in the office she went through to answer it. Patsy was ringing from her office, although the background noise indicated that business was still booming.

'About the jacket,' said Patsy. 'It was for you, wasn't it?'

'Yes,' said Alice.

'Well, I knew it was, of course. He asked me to hold it for him before you went, and when he came back for it I offered it to him for nothing, because it seemed the least I could do, but he wasn't having that; he insisted on paying. I say,' said Patsy, 'isn't he a stunner?'

'Yes, he is,' said Alice.

'Shop's still full,' said Patsy gleefully. 'Of course I know it won't go on like this, but it's a smashing start, and Granny Rosa's in her element. I hope she won't decide to carry on in the caravan. I don't think you can do that sort of thing without a licence, can you? And Mum and Dad wouldn't like it one bit.'

Alice could see that Granny Rosa coming out of retirement might be an embarrassment. She was a colourful character and it wouldn't be the first time she had stirred things up. Alice asked, 'Does she have the gift, the sight, whatever you call it?'

'I suppose she has,' said Patsy. 'She was on the road with the fair for forty-odd years doing her stuff, and she still comes out sometimes with things that frighten folk half to death. But she likes frightening folk; you know that.'

Alice had known the family ever since her father was a PR officer for the market and she was a child. She knew that Granny Rosa had once been a fortune-teller and that she could be a 'right old witch'. In the shop Alice had thought that most of her readings were just a party piece, chattering and flattering like an old fairground pro, but when she had grabbed Alice's arm it was different. There had been an urgency in her voice and her eyes, as though she could see the danger she spoke of. It had disturbed Alice then, and it did again now, taking the form of a slight headache, so that she went back into the kitchen pushing her hair off her forehead.

'What are you doing this afternoon?' Ivan asked her, and she said, without stopping to think,

'I might go for a walk.'

'Where?'

'I don't know, but it's been a busy day so far; I could do with some fresh air.'

'How about showing me where the toll-house used to be?'

After a little hesitation she said, 'All right.' She probably would have gone over the hills anyway; there was no place better for lifting a headache. And she wouldn't mind company. They could stride out together.

He was easier to be with this time. The tension seemed to be in abeyance, as if a truce had been declared. It hadn't but she was no longer uneasy about sitting beside him, not sure what he would say next so that she was on her guard all the time.

When he was silent so was she, and it didn't matter. It was comfortable. When she looked at him he smiled at her, and again she got the feeling that their smiles were like touching. That made her smile again as she was parking the car on the little slip-road at the foot of the hills. Good grief, she thought, I've met a man I could be intimate with across a crowded room.

She asked, 'Did you go this way?' It was the route she had described for him—only yesterday, was it?— and he had followed her directions.

They walked again up into the low-lying hills, taking a path that often vanished under the rough grass, through a wooded area, and out again to pass the old mine, with its tail chimney and rusting wheel.

She usually walked up here alone, but he was a good companion, not talking much, but in tune with her and the countryside. When it started to rain she held up her face, checking that the first drops were not imagination, and asked, 'Do we turn back?'

'Well, do we?'

'The toll-house isn't far, what's left of it.'

'Let's see the toll-house.'

'This will blow over,' she said, fairly confident because although the sky was grey the clouds were only slightly darker. 'And we're walking along Penny Lane now.' Although there was no sign of a lane in the shallow valley.

Alice walked on. 'It went between the two villages— our town was a village then. Horse-drawn carts used it, and there was a gate across. That's long gone— more than seventy years gone—but it was here.' She stopped. 'And the house was right under the oak tree.'

The oak tree looked good for another hundred years, but the one-storey cottage had almost vanished under gorse and shrubs, creepers and tall-growing grass. She walked through the gap where the door had hung. The wall remains were only few bricks high; there was no woodwork left, no windows, no roof except the spreading boughs of the tree. She had not stepped inside the walls for years, but she remembered the simple pattern of the cottage.

She said, 'It was just two rooms, one behind the other, and at the turn of the century the toll-keeper and his wife reared a family of seven in here.'

'Hard times.'

She agreed. Hard times for most in those days, but these children had at least had the freedom of the hills. There would have been chickens and a pig in a sty and vegetables grown in the garden. Others had had it worse. Under the roof of the twisted boughs she looked around her, and Ivan said, 'Penny for them.'

A penny toll. 'For what?' she asked.

'For your thoughts.'

How did he know she was thinking, not just looking? But she didn't mind telling him. No one else had known. No one else had asked. 'I used to come up here when I was much younger and make up stories—plays, I suppose you'd call them—about the toll-keeper's family. Four boys, three girls, they were, and I used to pretend I was one of the girls.

'I wasn't sorry for them; I thought it would be marvellous to be part of a family like that living here.'

'Were you a lonely child?'

'Not really. I had lots of friends, but I was an only child, and for a while this was my favourite game.'

'It was a lonely playground.'

There was no one else around now, and the grey skies over the silent hills made a gloomy picture, but she said, 'I only came in daylight, and of course it was a summer game. Things seemed to be different then; the pit was working and the miners came this way. There are still hikers and folk walking dogs. It never seemed to be lonely.'

Her mother had always been delicate, needing rest and quiet, and Alice had often peopled her own life with lively imaginary playmates. She had grown out of that when her mother died and responsibilities had crowded in on her. Now, far from wanting to be part of a crowd, she valued privacy above most things.

This wasn't a cottage any more—it never had been in her memory, only in her imagination—but under the shelter of the great tree it was a lair, out of the rain. Ivan took off his jacket and put it over the remains of the wall, and she sat down beside him.

She had used to do this, looking out through the 'open door' waiting to hear the clip-clop of horses' hooves, when her father the toll-keeper, who looked just like her real father except that he was dressed differently, would hurry out to collect the toll and unlock the gate.

That was years ago. She had almost forgotten the summer when she was the toll-keeper's daughter with brothers and sisters wherever she looked.

'Do you have any more relations?' Ivan was asking her.

'No. After my mother died it was just my father and myself.'

'The macho man?'

'Yes.' She could imagine him chuckling, hearing himself described like that. 'He was a good man,' she said. 'A good father.' Her mother had been gentle and loving too; she had been a cherished child. 'How are your parents?' she asked. 'Do you still have them?'

'I never did.' She was still and quietly attentive after that. 'I was dumped on a doorstep, yelling my head off, and brought up in an orphanage.'

How awful, she thought, although he was successful and wanting for nothing now, and he didn't sound sorry for himself. She asked, 'How did you get your name?' and he laughed.

'Ivan the Terrible, because I rarely stopped yelling, and Blackmore came out of the phone book. That could have been worse.'

'You'd have changed it if it had been,' she said. 'What happened next? How did you get where you are?'

'After I got educated——' he grinned at her and she wondered who his teachers had been, what they had taught him '—I hoboed around and then I wrote my first book.'

'*The Intruder*?' That headed the list in the library book.

'Yes. I used characters and stories I'd picked up along the way, and it did nicely. From then on I've carried on.'

Knowing nothing of your roots or forebears would mean that everything you did would be venturing into uncertain territory. 'And you found you were a born writer,' she said with a half-smile. 'Perhaps your father was a poet.'

He laughed again. 'Or a navvy with the gift of the gab. I'm handy with a shovel too.'

'Don't you want to know?' She would. She was alone now, but she had loving memories, and her home with the family mementoes was her refuge.

'No,' he said, without bitterness, but as though he just wasn't interested, and she could not understand that. She would have been desperate to trace somebody who could tell her something about her mother or father. 'You're not too hot at the weather-forecasting, are you?' he said.

The rain hadn't blown over. It was driving down now, hard and straight, and the pale grey skies had darkened with the threat of plenty more where this was coming from.

They were dry so far. The rain had not yet seeped through the massive tangle of boughs overhead.

Perhaps it never would, and if they stayed here they could sit out the downpour. By then night might have fallen and the moon and stars would be out.

Or would they? An afternoon like this could turn into a pitch-dark night when the hills would be a minefield of rabbit holes and subsidence cracks, and the risk of a twisted ankle would be the least of your worries.

She said, 'I've changed my mind. It isn't blowing over; it's set in. And we're going to get very wet, because we shall do no good sitting here.'

'I'm not so sure about that.' He had an arm around her shoulders and it would have been pleasant to stay huddled together in this little lair through the dark night. They might have shared more than confidences before the dawn, and that might be sensationally satisfying but not very sensible.

She stood up reluctantly. 'Let's make a run for it.'

He stood up too and got into his jacket and asked, 'What was your name when you were the toll-keeper's daughter?'

'Alice.'

He looked down at her for a moment, as though he was trying to imagine the child she had been. Her appearance had not changed that much. She was taller, of course. She had had long hair until her mother died—her mother had liked it long; she had loved to brush the pale silken waves. At thirteen Alice had cut her hair to a bob, and it had stayed more or less that way ever since, although for years of course she had had it professionally styled.

She shivered suddenly and said, 'This is crazy, but they were real to me in those days, this family I invented.' She could remember the names she had given them. She said, 'Goodbye,' as they stepped out from the shelter of the tree, and almost believed she could hear whispers in the rustle of the wind in the branches.

Almost at once she slowed down and found herself smiling because Ivan was smiling. There was nothing to be gained by running; they would be drenched before they reached the car, no matter how fast they went. He took her hand and they sauntered along together while the rain sluiced down on them as if they were under a waterfall.

Her make-up had gone within minutes. She felt the mascara in her eyes briefly, but it was washed out as quickly as it had floated in, and she knew that the rain running down her face and her neck, trickling right to the skin of her stomach, was removing cream and colour, leaving her shining like a scrubbed child.

She was feeling ridiculously young, splashing along without a care. There might have been a touch of hysteria in this, but it was mostly elation that had her laughing and almost jumping in puddles.

Her hair was soaked. If she shook her head the raindrops would fly in all directions, like a dog coming out of a river. She must look an absolute fright, and he couldn't have been wetter if he had jumped in the river. Two right guys, and she thought it was the funniest thing that had happened to her in years.

They rushed at the car and fell in as she opened the doors. Outside the rain pelted the window-panes and inside they squelched as they moved. There was a packet of tissues between the seats and he took out a handful and tried to mop her face, but her hair fell over her eyes in a dripping curtain and she said, 'You've got to be joking,' and then she was giggling again. 'We'd better get home,' she said.

He was laughing too. 'Nobody else is going to want us in this state, although a cleaner pair would be hard to find.'

Her hands were sticky on the gear lever and her boots seemed to have shrunk several sizes. Steam seemed to rise from them as the car warmed up, and when she had it in the garage she said, 'I was starting a headache before we started out. It's washed that away; we're lucky to have our heads left.'

'Are you all right?'

'I'm fine.' The dark thatch of his hair looked wilder than ever, and she wanted to touch the damp skin of his face. She said gaily, 'I must be a case of arrested mental development. First I start babbling about games I played as a child, and then I really enjoyed this. Dancing in the rain wasn't in it.'

'You're not as fragile as you look.'

He smiled down at her as she unbuttoned her sodden coat in the hall and she said, 'I'm not fragile, just pasty-faced.' Then she sniffed, because raindrops were dripping off her nose, and said, 'But if I don't get into a hot bath I could turn fragile.'

'See you in twenty minutes?'

'Make it half an hour. Then come down and we'll have a hot drink.'

He went upstairs and she turned on the electric fire in the living-room before she ran her bath and peeled off her rain-soaked clothing. She was damp to the skin. Everything was for the washing-machine, and she had a moment of fleeting amusement wondering how Ivan Blackmore would deal with Miss Pringle's machine in his kitchen. Outer clothes would need a dry-cleaners, but what would he do with his smalls? Then she remembered that he had been shifting for himself for years and was probably every bit as capable as Miss Pringle had been.

The bath was bliss. She poured in a generous helping of bath-oil and wallowed in the soft scented water, pampering herself like a lady of leisure or a teenager getting ready for a very important date.

She was neither, of course, but her spirits were buoyant, as though the cloudbursts had washed away the reserve of years and made her a girl again.

Getting caught in a downpour over the hills with anyone else might have had them laughing and running, young and strong and heading for warmth and shelter, and their ordeal would have had its comic side, but with Ivan it had been hilarious. She had felt as if she were dancing half the time, smiling up at him, keeping hold of his hand and tasting rain like cool kisses on her lips.

She washed her hair and got into undies and a slip dress, and her towelling robe because her hair was dripping, wrapping her head in a towel and not bothering with shoes—she often went barefoot in her home after working hours.

He was in the living-room, wearing jeans and an Aran sweater, and she thought, You could be a Cornish fisherman. When he had said he came from Cornwall, did he mean he was abandoned there or that Cornwall was a more recent home?

'Kettle's boiling,' he said. 'What do we do with it?'

'Coffee? We could spike it with whiskey. I've got half a bottle.'

So they made mugs of Irish coffee without the cream, and she began to towel her hair, sitting on a cushion in front of the fire. When he took the towel from her she wasn't surprised, nor that he did it without saying anything; it seemed a natural thing to do.

She sat, hugging her knees, head bowed and eyes closed. Later they would eat, go out or stay in and rustle up something from her stock cupboard, but for now she was adrift in dreamy, dopey contentment. The scalp massage was more relaxing than any salon treatment. Through the soft thickness of the towel the moving fingertips sent little whirls of pleasure through the nerves of her neck and shoulders.

She murmured, 'You've got a lovely touch with a towel,' and he said,

'Are you expecting a caller?'

'What?' Her head came up as she pushed the towel from her face.

Another face stared in through the glass of the French windows. It was dark outside now, but Robin was close enough to be recognisable, and Alice swore softly. She would have liked to mouth, Go away, and get up and pull the curtains close together.

'Hadn't we better see what he wants?' said Ivan.

CHAPTER FIVE

'I KNOW what he wants,' Alice muttered. 'Drat the man.'

She retied the belt of her robe and padded across. Friends used both the front door and this back entrance, but it was months since Robin Hailey had called at her home, and with the glass between them she was still tempted to pull the curtains and shut him out.

She hadn't asked him to come. She had been feeling relaxed and cosseted, and he had already interrupted what might have been the prelude to something even better. But of course she couldn't shut him out. All she could do was let him in and then get rid of him. She opened the doors just wide enough and he edged in sheepishly, apologising, 'Sorry I've called at an awkward time.'

Any time would have been awkward when she didn't want to see him at all. 'Not particularly,' she said crisply. 'This is Robin Hailey,' she told Ivan, who had already seen him once today, looking wounded in the precinct. 'Ivan Blackmore.' She waved a hand towards Ivan and thought she seemed to be doing a lot of this.

The men acknowledged each other. The rain had flattened Robin's hair. He looked wet, a drip, and she could see the resemblance between him and Martin. Ivan seemed another breed, someone from another planet. 'I'll—get another coffee,' he said, and she knew he was finding this amusing.

She didn't think she was. She wanted to say, Don't go, but he had, and Robin stood there sighing.

'I went into the shop, but they said you'd left,' he said. Patsy hadn't told her that; perhaps he had gone in after the phone call. 'Seeing you again,' he said, 'I thought I'd try again.'

Now why did he think that? What encouragement had she given him in those few seconds? Then he sighed even deeper. 'I never thought Martin Royston would last, but I'm too late, aren't I?'

He thought she was off with Martin and on with Ivan, but whatever was happening she could never take on Robin again, so she just said, 'Yes.'

'I don't know him, do I?'

Robin meant, Is he local? and Alice said, 'He's Miss Pringle's tenant. The upstairs apartment.' She added, to fill the silence that followed, 'She's gone to Australia,' and Robin tried for a cynical grin.

'That's far enough. How long have you known him?'

Alice said quietly, 'It seems a long time,' and he knew it was hopeless. Alice's elusiveness had always fascinated him, but when she withdrew like this he had no way of reaching her.

She took him to the front door. His car was a little way down the road, although there was parking space outside her house. He must have walked up in the rain, getting the courage to knock on her door, only to find her cosily settled in with another man.

She was sorry for him there, but irritated too, because what was wrong with the girl he was dating? For one thing she was several inches shorter; that might give him more confidence. Even barefoot, Alice was almost as tall as he was. He and his girlfriend both worked for an insurance broker, so they had an interest in stocks and shares in common. And she was pretty.

But he held Alice's hand on the doorstep and promised, 'I'll always be waiting,' and she thought that the drama had gone on long enough.

She said, 'Of course you won't. I'm not right for you.' Nor was he right for her. Nor were any of them. She had always played with losers, but the winner she had come across now could be out of her league.

'You're the most beautiful woman I know,' Robin said huskily, and she had a mad impulse to pull a gargoyle face and shake her still damp hair like Medusa's snakes, because he hadn't a clue what she was really like.

She said, 'You have no idea how ugly I can be,' and shut the door with a louder bang than she had intended.

Ivan came out of the kitchen enquiring, 'How many more are there?'

Her ex-boyfriends had been rather underfoot lately, but there was no need for him to sound as if she were working her way through the books of an escort agency.

'My score's below average,' she said, and compared to most of her friends' it was.

She went back into the living-room, leaving the towel on the floor and kneeling in front of the fire. The heat from the electric bars was like the sun on the crown of her head, as she went on with what she had been saying. 'But, living in the same town, we're bound to cross paths occasionally. You move on, I suppose.'

'Yes.'

He had followed her into the room now and he went to the windows and drew the curtains together, and she said, 'I'll remember to do that after tonight.' Looking down at her bare knees, she mused, 'I suppose he did realise I was dressed under this.'

'Did you tell him?' He was sitting back in the easy-chair now, and she turned to look up at him.

'I didn't think about it.'

'Does it matter?'

'Not a lot.' She grimaced. 'But Robin never was what you'd call discreet. If he got the wrong impression he could be telling somebody about it.'

Ivan laughed, and so did she, because it didn't matter. 'Maybe you should have come out of the kitchen and told him how platonic this is,' she gurgled.

'Lie to him?'

'Would it be a lie?'

'What else when we both know I'm hell-bent on seducing you?'

There might be some truth in that, but they were still fooling, and she teased with dancing eyes, 'It could be harder than you think.'

'I know. Granny Rosa was no help, and neither, if you'll forgive me for saying so, is this room.'

It was a pleasant room, the walls a pale peach and the big old carpet patterned in warm beige and apricot. She had left this room much as it had always been, replacing the old leather chesterfield with a single divan bed that doubled as a sofa, but keeping knick-knacks on the sideboard and china in the glass-fronted cupboard.

'Too cramped?' she said. 'Too much clutter?' She looked around as if she was considering it as a seduction setting, then said solemnly, 'I can see that getting too abandoned would be risking knocking something over. How about your apartment?'

'Too much Miss Pringle,' he said. 'There are some very disapproving chairs in the living-room, and I can't see myself giving much of a performance in her bed.'

She gave a hoot of laughter. Miss Pringle's bedroom was one background in which she found it almost impossible to imagine him. 'So I'm safe so long as I stay in this house?' she said.

'Unfortunately, yes. How about us leaving town for a few days?'

'I've just come back from holiday; I'm not due for another break for ages.'

'No?' They were talking nonsense, but it was a fact that he went where he liked but she was held here. Now he asked, 'Have you always lived in this house?'

'I was born here. I sold the top floor when my father died.'

'You've never wanted to try anywhere else?'

'Why should I?' This was her home; her work was here. So were her friends and her clients. 'It suits me.' She had moved a little from the fire and was looking straight across at him. 'Have you never found anywhere you wanted to stay?'

'Not for long.'

So it probably was not a home in Cornwall. 'Like a six-month lease?' she suggested.

'About that.'

Six months seemed about how long her relationships lasted, so if this one took off the lease and the love-affair should come to an end more or less together. A neat and tidy arrangement. But suddenly the warmth of the fire was not reaching her, as though a chill wind had crept into the room.

She forced herself to keep smiling, joking, 'No, I can't imagine making love among Miss Pringle's furniture. Unless we closed our eyes.'

'That I couldn't promise.' He looked at her with the admiration she had seen in his eyes before, but she knew he was not thinking that she was the most beautiful woman he had ever seen.

She would have liked to ask, Who was? Your ex, Felicity, what was she like? Tall, short, dark, fair? You seem to know a lot about the men in my life, except for my father, who didn't have a macho bone in his body. But I know nothing about your women, and unless there are some clues in your books I'm not likely to find out anything.

'Well,' she said, 'I'm staying put right here, so seduction's out for now, is it?'

'Looks like it.'

'All the same, I'll remember the gypsy's warning. Granny Rosa might have been wrong about your easy start in life, but she knows a dangerous man when she sees one.'

'But not a dangerous woman?'

'What?'

'Still waters running deep.'

He meant her, and she said gaily, 'We all have our secrets.' She had her secrets, but she was not dangerous. Calling an end to love-affairs that had no future might have hurt some male pride, but not too deeply, she was sure of that. She was no real danger to anyone. She asked, 'Do you want food?' and was surprised when he said,

'No, thanks; I'd better be going.'

She had thought they would spend what was left of the evening together, although she had no reason to take that for granted, nor for feeling disappointed. This had not been a date, just a walk over the hills and a chat by the fire.

'Goodnight, then.' She smiled up, and he went down on his heels to cup her chin and kiss her lips. Again she got a charge that took her breath away, so that she gasped before she could gulp, 'That was a good-night kiss?'

'Of course it was.' He got up. 'When I try seducing you I do hope you'll notice the difference.'

'Oh, I'm sure I will.'

She stayed where she was for a while, drying her hair and wondering why Ivan's light touch went so much deeper than the passionate lovemaking of other men.

There was no answer to that—it was just how it was—and she got up at last to go into the kitchen and heat a tin of mushroom soup and make buttered toast, and to fetch his book out of the drawer in her desk.

The title that headed the list inside—the book he had written while he was 'hoboing around'—was called *The Intruder*, and that was ironic when she had started off suspecting him of being the intruder who had broken into her home and her life. A coincidence, of course, a joke in its way, but not one she would be explaining to anybody.

This book was *Dark Refuge*, and she was still reading it after midnight, with her eyes starting to smart about people trapped in the maelstrom of a civil war, and she was convinced that these men and women were real, that it had all happened or was happening. The writing was brilliant, at times brutal, and when she switched off the light she expected her dreams to be troubled.

It had not been a book for bedtime, leaving her mind over-active, although her eyes were tired. She lay still, trying not to think about the story or the man, but she couldn't have been too successful, because when she woke for the first time a few hours later she had tossed off most of the bedclothes.

She couldn't remember her dreams, but vague nightmarish images were still in her mind, so that she was shaking as she reached to pull the tangle of sheets and duvet over her.

It was ages before she could get back to sleep, and when she woke again, more or less at her usual time, she knew she had gone on dreaming, because she woke so scared. There was nothing in real life to scare her so it had to be a dream, but for her first few conscious moments she seemed to be running for her life, fleeing from something or somebody.

She soon stopped that, sitting up and shaking her head to clear it. All in all she had had a restless night, and she picked up the book from the floor, and put it with others on a shelf, firmly resolved to read no more Ivan Blackmore just before bedtime.

Her morning was full, keeping her in the office, and when she answered the phone to Karen she was prepared to be civil, but she couldn't spare much time for small talk with a woman she didn't much like.

Karen was presumably still after Ivan, and what he did was up to him; Alice was not the go-between. When Karen started, 'About Ivan Blackmore…' Alice drew in breath to say, I am very busy, only Karen went on, 'I'm not one to complain—nobody could say I'm not broad-minded—but his manners are appalling.'

'His what?' Alice gasped.

Karen's voice was going up and down, as if she was quivering with outrage. 'I just rang him on Miss Pringle's number and said I hoped he'd be happy here, and it would be nice to have him staying in our road, and do you know what he said to me?'

Alice didn't need to guess, because Karen was going to tell her, but Karen suddenly became very genteel after a little clearing of the throat. 'He told me——' another cough '—to—something off.'

'What? Oh!' Alice was surprised that Karen felt it necessary to censor that. She would have thought her quite capable of getting the words out, and she knew it was what several women had wanted to say to her. 'Oh, dear!' said Alice.

'That wasn't very nice, was it?' Karen was getting primmer by the minute.

'No,' Alice had to agree. 'Ivan Blackmore is a lot of things, but nice is not one of them.'

'And I hope you know what you're doing with him,' Karen snapped. 'Because he doesn't seem your sort at all.'

How would you know, Alice might have asked, when you and I had only exchanged a few words until he turned up? But those who knew her well would say the same, and of course she didn't know what she was doing with him. Everything was just happening; she wasn't planning it. She couldn't imagine anyone getting the chance to plan his life, but she said, 'I see what you mean,' and Karen put down the phone.

Not my fault, Alice said to it, and chuckled with cheerful malice as she went on with her work.

Ivan came into the office as she was listening to the one o'clock news on the radio and said, 'Time off for lunch?'

'Not too much; I've got a busy afternoon.'

'So have I; I thought we could eat in Miss Pringle's kitchen.'

She got up. 'I had a call from Karen.'

'Snap,' he said.

'After yours. She rang me to complain about your appalling behaviour.'

He went ahead up the stairs, asking over his shoulder, 'And what did she want you to do about it?'

'What I am doing, I suppose—register her complaint.' She tutted, with mock-disapproval. 'Fine language to use to a lady who only wanted to say welcome to the road.'

'She thinks you're a lady too.' On the landing a savoury smell was coming from the kitchen; Alice breathed it in as she followed him to the stove. 'She said, "Do you have to bring Alice? She's quite a lady, but so provincial, if you know what I mean."'

'She's hardly jet set herself,' said Alice. 'And bring me where? Where were you going?'

'Over to her place. She's got this little recipe she knows I'd be crazy about.'

'I think I've heard it mentioned before,' said Alice. 'Ready any time, is it?'

'So I gathered, but her timing was off this morning. I was getting down to work and then the phone rang, and like a fool I answered it, and got this Marilyn Monroe impression, all squeaks and gasps.'

'If you'd told her she sounded like Marilyn Monroe she'd have been happier.'

'I didn't want her happy.' There was a pan of spaghetti boiling and another pan of sauce. He gave the sauce a stir, frowning, as if he were discovering something surprising in it. 'I was annoyed at being interrupted. I was going to cut her off and leave the phone off so I wasn't disturbed again, when she said, "Don't bring Alice; Alice is so provincial." Now what's wrong with being provincial?'

'Not a thing,' said Alice. Except that Karen had meant narrow-minded and dull; Karen was being snide.

'But that was when I lost patience with her.'

'And told her to—was it shove off?'

'Near enough.'

'She couldn't bring herself to repeat your actual words.'

He grinned. 'What a sheltered life she must have led. So much for you being the provincial lady.' And she burst out laughing.

She could understand how a silly interruption would irritate him, but hearing that it was the crack at her that had angered him was something to smile about. He wasn't telling her to impress her; he hadn't realised it himself until now. Without that, Karen's invitation would have been turned down flat, but instinctively he had resented her sneering at Alice and seen her off in no uncertain terms.

Alice could have hugged him, it was such a comforting compliment, but if you grabbed this one you could find yourself being held away, and Alice was no easy touch herself. So she went on smiling and peered into the saucepan and asked, 'What's this?'

'A little recipe I know you'll be crazy about,' he said, quoting Karen and making her laugh again.

'Specially for me? Was it much trouble?'

'You don't create masterpieces like this in five minutes. Say seven.'

There was a breakfast bar in Miss Pringle's kitchen, but her stools were several inches too short for Ivan's legs. After they had drained the spaghetti and dished it up and spooned the sauce over, Alice sat on her stool and he perched with knees bent on his.

'Onions, tomatoes, prawns, mussels, clams,' she identified, and, sniffing, 'And garlic. It's spaghetti marinara.'

'Is it?'

'Don't you know?'

'I stocked up the larder this morning and this seemed as good a combination as any, but I should warn you my sauces are never the same twice. Spaghetti marinara—and why not?'

'Sprinkle with chopped parsley and serve with Parmesan cheese,' she intoned. 'You can rely on my sauces; I'm a cook who goes by the book.'

In fact she had invented many a tasty dish with whatever came to hand, and he said, 'No parsley or Parmesan. Can you force it down without?'

'I'll try.' She twirled a strand of spaghetti round her fork, dipped it in the sauce, and started eating. 'It's good; it's delicious. This is *nice*.'

'I think so,' he said, and she had never felt so re-laxed and happy to be here, not even in Miss Pringle's time.

They talked about her morning. She was still on the interior design promotion, and he knew a young TV actress who was buying a house a few miles away who might be interested in their designs. A star client could be good publicity, and Alice touched wood and said, 'Do please ask her.'

They talked a little about his work. He was getting notes and research into order, and when her phone rang downstairs he said, 'Mine's still off the hook. I'll put it back after lunch. Are you answering yours?'

'If it matters they'll call again,' she said.

It was as if nobody could reach them up here, like being snug in the lair of the toll-keeper's cottage, cut off from the rest of the world.

They talked about what they would do after work, where they might go for their evening meal. Alice knew most of the local eating places. 'If we set off about seven,' she said, 'we'll get in almost anywhere this time of year. Or is there anywhere you like?'

'I haven't been here long enough to have a preference,' he said. 'Seven o'clock suits me.'

The phone started ringing again as she came downstairs, and now she hurried to catch it, then wished she hadn't. Martin was wanting an explanation. Surprise, surprise, Robin Hailey had been walking along the high street when Martin came out of his office at lunchtime, and had greeted him with, 'Welcome to the rejects club; it seems to happen to all of us sooner or later.'

Now Martin was sure there was an explanation. He knew that Hailey had been sore when Alice ended their affair and that he had always resented Martin, and why was he doing a peeping Tom through Alice's window last night? You couldn't put much reliance on what Robin Hailey said. But did she know what he was saying he'd seen?

'I know what he did see,' she said. 'Me, wearing a robe over my clothes because my hair was wet, and

Ivan drying my hair with a towel. X-certificate it wasn't, and if he's going round saying it was he's asking for trouble.'

Martin said quickly, 'Oh, I told him that. I told him that while we were on holiday you and I had practically named the day and I had the ring right here in my pocket.'

Alice did one of her silent screams. She was not sure which rumour was the more annoying—that she had been caught in some very heavy petting with a man she had just met, or that she was marrying Martin Royston.

In this small town both could be believed. She drew in a deep breath and said, 'Unless you want to look a fool, start denying the marriage bit. Say you said it to shut him up because he's an idiot. I am not getting married to you; I have told you that. I am not getting married, period.'

She hung up the phone and wondered whether, by evening, she would find this funny enough to tell it in a way that would make Ivan laugh. All she wanted to do now was bang Martin's and Robin's heads together, because between them they had landed her in a crazy situation.

Soon she would be getting phone calls: congratulations on her 'engagement' from those who knew Martin, and from those who had met Ivan—excluding Karen Morton—congratulations of a raunchier kind.

She was staying out of the office until she was through the screaming stage. If she met anyone face to face who had heard the gossip she would say that it was nonsense, but a succession of phone calls could only fuel her frustration.

Ivan was right about her choosing wimps. The last two were dim-wits as well. Robin couldn't see straight and Martin couldn't understand plain English. They might both be sensitive and caring, but at the moment their good points were heavily outweighed for Alice.

She called on a couple of clients—she had to contact them anyway, so it wasn't time wasted—and went into the newspaper offices to see what space they were giving to the launch of On the Wild Side.

There would be an advertisement feature that Alice had already written, stressing the romance of Patsy's Romany background, although Patsy had lived in a modern brick-built house since she was three years old. And in the photographic department Owen French was sitting alone at his desk.

He showed her the photographs. They had come out well. Ivan looked handsome and saturnine, and everyone around looked happy. There was a shot of Granny Rosa, reading the palm of a wide-eyed teenager; and the fortune-telling and Ivan Blackmore's appearance had turned the opening of Patsy's little shop into quite a local event.

Alice was more than satisfied with the coverage they could expect in Saturday's paper. 'Good-looking devil, isn't he?' said Owen, and she supposed he was looking at Ivan in the photograph she was holding. 'Not your usual sort of bloke.'

'I hardly know him.' That was part truth, part un-truth. It was less than a week that sometimes seemed nearer years. 'Tell me about him,' she said.

'Well, I only met him the once.' Owen's sharp features under his ginger hair were suddenly lit with a grin that made him look more pixie-like than ever. 'Hell of a thing, that was.'

'So why aren't you smiling?' said Alice.

'Wouldn't have missed it, though.' He picked up one of the photographs. 'Not bad,' he said. 'I'm not bad, but I've done better, and the best was when I met Blackmore.'

He leaned back in his chair, reminiscing. 'Year before last we went on holiday to California, Jess and the girls and me, and they stayed on with some relations we've got out there, while I took off for a few days driving into the desert.

'There was this small town—not much more than a settlement—called Jeremiah's Tree, and that was where I came across Blackmore. He was passing through, as I was, and we had a meal together, talked, and there was this earthquake.'

Alice blinked. 'Just like that?'

'Just like that,' said Owen, as if he had pulled off a conjuring trick. 'It's close to the San Andreas Fault, so shocks aren't that uncommon, but this was the worst they'd had there for forty years.'

Alice was impressed, and Owen warmed to his tale. 'I was scared witless, I can tell you. The road started making waves, buildings were cracking, cars were jumping up and down, everybody was running and screaming. They said it was all over in thirty seconds, but I still can't believe that. If Blackmore hadn't stayed cool I should have been screaming; I was that near panic.

'Well, we helped, getting the injured out. He's strong as a bull—what he was lifting was unbelievable—and it was a miracle nobody was badly hurt, and when we stood back and I said, "What do we do now?" he said, "You're a Pressman, aren't you? Take the pictures".'

Owen's grin was rueful this time. 'You know, I'd never thought of that. I'd been taking pictures everywhere, but not when the crunch came. I knew then I'm never going to be one of the greats. So I took the pictures—of the aftermath—and they were good, my best ever.'

'I'd like to see them,' said Alice, because Owen needed a boost and she was usually a kind-hearted girl.

'Bless you,' he said. 'You shall. Well, that's all I can tell you about him. He writes bloody well, but you'll know that anyway.'

Not till last night, thought Alice, when one of his books gave me nightmares...

They had been alone in this section of the department, but as another photographer came out of the dark-room Owen summed up, 'Some men can work and live on the edge because that's their kind of country. There aren't many of them; I don't know another like Blackmore. Not me, for sure; I doubt if I'll ever feel the earth move again.'

The junior photographer did a double take and Alice said, 'Remember me to Jess, and tell her there's a rumour about that Martin Royston and I are getting married. We're not.'

'Of course you're not,' said Owen. 'Not with Ivan Blackmore in your house.'

'And don't read too much into that either,' said Alice. She was out of the building before she remembered that she hadn't got round to denying the other rumour—Robin's account of what he thought he had seen through her window. But, as she had told Ivan, that didn't matter much.

* * *

Showering and changing to go out that night, Alice hovered over the silk jacket. It would be suitable for the evening ahead but she did rather fancy keeping the first wearing for an occasion. She didn't know what. Just when she went somewhere in style. Tonight she thought a pub with atmosphere would fit the bill, and there were plenty of those around.

In the end she wore sweater and trousers, both in jade-green the tapering trousers flattering her long, slim legs. The sweater's high roll collar framed her face, and she slung on several thin gold chains for a glitzy touch.

When Ivan came downstairs she went out into the hall and asked, 'Will I do?'

'You know you'll do.'

She supposed so. 'So let's go,' she said. 'On the cheap tonight, I thought. Is that all right?'

'You're the guide.' As she went towards the door leading into the garage he said, 'Shall we take my car?' He had the garage just around the corner that Miss Pringle had rented, and where her elderly Morris Minor had stood was a gleaming Jaguar.

'Very classy,' said Alice. She could tell in the first few minutes that he was a skilful driver, and she said, 'I can see why you prefer your car to mine.'

'Nothing wrong with your car. Nor with the question mark.'

'You said it suited me—Miss Enigma. You're the open book, I suppose.'

'I wouldn't say that.' His grin was slow and easy. 'But you're welcome between my covers any time.'

The *double entendre* was a joke, but he did use the people he met in his books, and she wondered if she might feature in the future. A smile came with the thought that if she was going to turn up, under an alias, she might as well give him something spectacularly hair-raising to remember.

The inn had stood on these crossroads since the days when stage coaches had stopped here, and through two hundred years of repairs and restorations had managed to maintain much of the original character. The brickwork had mellowed into warm nut-brown, and lights gleamed behind the diamond-paned windows.

As they got out of the car Ivan looked up at the swinging sign which read 'The Five Crosses', and queried, 'Five?'

'It used to be The Four Crosses,' Alice explained, 'but in the 1880s some joker painted it "Five". The fifth cross the landlord had to bear was his wife—she was a notorious nag—and the local boozers thought that it was so funny it stayed that way.'

Alice had always felt sorry for the wife, wondering why she was nagging. Now she said, 'And what a life it must have been for her after that when every stage-coach unloaded somebody who wanted to know why "Five". I hope she took off.'

'You would have done,' said Ivan, and her hand was through his arm and she was laughing with him.

'At a rate of knots,' she said.

The ground floor was a large public bar, with sepia-coloured photographs and even older sketches and bill posters on the walls beneath the black-beamed ceiling. Alice headed for the wide wooden staircase leading up to the restaurant, passing a group of leather-jacketed bikers who were knocking back the ale. They had never seen her before, but a chorus of ear-splitting whistles rose as she climbed the stairs, and then Ivan, who was beside her, stopped and turned and looked down.

They were no physical threat, although by the time she had reached the top of the stairs they would have been loudly discussing her bodywork in coarse and colourful detail. A girl as tall and as striking as Alice did get that treatment. She hated it and she ignored it, but this time it didn't happen.

They went on grinning, but nobody said a word, and in the tall man beside her, smiling and waiting, hands loose and eyes watchful, she sensed more ice-cold menace than in the half-dozen loudmouths below.

She thought incredulously, Six to one and they're scared of him. They believe that the first to mouth off will be hurt, and so do I. And she went quickly up the rest of the stairs, because she did not want that.

Not even a final wolf-whistle followed, and in the dining-room Ivan said, 'Friends of yours?'

'Do you mind? Strangers in town.' A waitress came to meet them, giving Alice a friendly hello and signalling approval of her companion. Sophie's parents owned The Five Crosses. Alice had often been in here with Martin Royston, and, whoever this was, Sophie thought he was a big improvement on Martin, a real knock-out.

There were plenty of empty tables and she seated them at one as far from others as possible, because if she had been on a date with a man like this herself she would have liked some privacy. Then she waited while they studied the menu. Alice knew it by heart; it was a regular tariff, with ham and eggs the speciality.

Ivan settled for that and Alice chose the seafood platter, and Sophie thought he had such a sexy voice that she got him to repeat the order to hear him say it again. When it arrived, Alice saw that he had two rounds of ham instead of the usual one.

'Sophie's done you proud,' she said. 'You get double rations because she likes the look of you, and I get sexually harassed going up the stairs. Not much equality in that.'

'Is this a double?'

'It is.'

'We must come again.'

'I'm glad you approve. It's an interesting place.' She gestured around the big room. 'They used to have cock fights in here.'

'*What*?'

'Oh, about the time they were changing Four Crosses to Five.' She ate a prawn and said gaily, 'I'm a mine of information. My father helped to write a book on local legends, ghosting for the vicar. Inquests, too; this is where inquests were held. Accidents, usually, mostly from the pit. The body would be lying on a trestle-table ready for the inquest next day, and if it was a cock-fighting day today they'd all turn up as mourners, whether they knew them or not. Then they'd cover the body with a sheet, push the table out of the way against the wall, and get on with the cock-fighting.' She shuddered. 'Horrible lot, weren't they?'

'Your ancestors?'

'I hope not.'

She nibbled on a long, thin chip of potato, and he said, 'There are advantages in being an orphan.'

She was an orphan. Her mother and father were dead; there was a headstone with their names in the churchyard. But he could have living parents some-where. He travelled world-wide, researched records and memories, met countless people. He could have followed the clues, and she said, 'You really aren't interested in finding out——?'

'No,' he said, so finally that she couldn't go on, no matter how intrigued she was. So she started telling him about Robin and Martin, and that was so absurd that she was laughing as she spoke, and when somebody patted her shoulder she nearly choked.

'Whoops, sorry,' said Ros, from the estate agency of Burroughs and Son.

Alice coughed and Ivan said, 'Hello again,' to Ros and the young man with her, Jason Burroughs, the 'and Son' and Ros's boyfriend.

'We thought it had to be you when Sophie described who Alice was with,' said Ros, and Alice thought, I'd like to have heard that description. 'Everything satisfactory?' asked Ros, adding archly, 'With the apartment, I mean.'

'Very satisfactory,' said Ivan, and Alice said,

'Join us?' It was a table for four, and she didn't want to give them the idea that this was an exclusive twosome. They hesitated and then Ros said, 'Just for coffee, then, eh?'

Sophie, who had come up behind, took the order, and Jason asked Ivan how he was liking it here. They'd heard he had opened a shop in the precinct on Tuesday, and if he was ever considering somewhere more permanent than a short lease they had several other interesting properties on their books.

'If I should need an estate agent,' said Ivan, 'I'll get in touch.'

'Don't hold your breath,' Alice murmured. 'By the way, have you heard any good gossip lately?'

'Like what?' Ros leaned forward eagerly, and Alice guessed it had not yet reached Ros, so she summed up for her,

'Like Martin and I have named the day.'

'You never.'

'No, but Martin told somebody we had, and it could be doing the rounds.'

Jason was describing his star property, and Ros, under the impression that Ivan's attention was fixed on Jason, mouthed, Are you having trouble with Martin? Alice shrugged. 'You'll cope,' said Ros. 'You always do.'

She risked a sideways glance at Ivan, who would be why Alice was dumping Martin, and met his amused look. It didn't take much to keep Ros babbling; embarrassment did it now. 'I was just saying that Alice can cope with anything; nothing ever fazes Alice. I wish I were like that; I wish I could keep my cool.'

Ivan raised an eyebrow at Alice and she thought, That's me, with everybody but you. You are the only one who struck sparks from the beginning.

She smiled and shook her head, and Ros went on, 'Honestly, it's something I really envy her. I always have. We went to school together,' she informed the men. 'We've always known each other and I've never known Alice to panic about anything. I remember once——' her voice took on the thrilling quality of someone with a riveting tale to tell '—there was a break-in at Alice's house. She was all alone and she was tied up while they ransacked the place.'

Nothing short of screaming Shut up, would have halted Ros, but Alice managed to look bored, her hands clenching together beneath the table in a vice-like grip.

'I would have been so scared,' said Ros, 'but Alice was cool as a cucumber. She knew her father was due back with some friends any time, and they did come and the men ran away. Her father was very upset, but Alice just laughed the whole thing off. Wasn't that fantastic?'

'No, it wasn't,' Alice said quickly. 'The break-in was a bore, of course—he took things; I was mad about that—but I wasn't really alone. I knew my father and his friends would be coming.'

Ros was no longer clear on details. After four years that was to be expected, and break-ins, even in small towns, were commoner than they used to be. Alice's was history. She wanted it played down and forgotten, not talked about. Jason said it was a rotten thing to happen to anyone. Somebody he knew had been burgled four times in twelve months. Motorways were making the getaways easier.

Ivan asked, 'What was taken?'

'From our house?' said Alice, and when he nodded, 'I've forgotten most of it.' That was not so. She would always remember everything. 'Oh, the usual: silverware, money, credit cards, jewellery. It wasn't a great haul; we didn't have anything that valuable. I remember my mother's string of pearls, some rings and things. And my great-grandmother's Mizpah brooch. That was the thing I was sorriest to lose; I was very fond of that.'

'What's a Mizpah brooch?' asked Ros.

Alice said, 'They were Victorian keepsakes, in gold, two hearts engraved, ''The Lord watch over thee and me when we are absent one from the other''.'

'That's sweet,' said Ros.

'Yes,' said Alice. Her fingers were still locked. She had been clenching them so tightly that when she pulled them apart they were numb and it was a few seconds before she could pick up her fork.

They stayed a foursome for the rest of the evening, with Ros and Jason chattering away and Ivan keeping the talk going. Alice watched him and wondered whether his interest in what they were saying was one of the tricks of his trade, although it seemed genuine enough.

She would have been happy to say goodnight to them earlier, but they showed no signs of leaving, and when goodbyes were said it was in the car park and not too far off midnight.

In the car she said, 'It's a small world round here. There aren't many places where I won't meet someone I know.'

'Say the word,' he said, 'and we'll take off,' and she laughed softly and thought how marvellous it would be to leave everything behind and go without a care.

'The word's home,' she said. 'Straight home. My working day starts right after breakfast.'

She was beginning to feel drowsy, and in the hall at the bottom of the stairs she tried to stifle a yawn. 'Sleep well,' he said and again he kissed her, lightly and affectionately, and again the kiss tingled to her nerve-ends.

'You too,' she said. 'See you tomorrow.' She went into her living-room and heard the door close at the top of the stairs and then she gasped, 'Wow!'

* * *

Next day she worked without a break. Ivan looked into her kitchen as she was drinking her first coffee of the day and said he'd be out till evening. He didn't say where and she didn't ask, but what she had decided to do was arrange some free time on Saturday. Sundays she usually took off, and two free days should mean they could do something together.

Of course he might have his own plans, but, if he hadn't, two friends could be getting to know each other better. It would be nothing hurried; there were months ahead of coming back here at night and keeping her head because she wasn't risking losing control in dealing with a tiger. But she did have a few ideas where they could go, and when she saw him this evening she would trot them out.

She was on the phone when he came back. He put his head round the door of the office and said, 'Come up when you're through,' and she signalled that she would.

She finished her phone call and she made some notes and took her time, because she shouldn't be rushing upstairs. She was a cool lady, showing signs of infatuation which were bothersome to say the least, and confusing after so long being in charge of every aspect of her emotional life.

I don't even know if I like him, she thought. I don't like ruthless men, and I am sure that he is one. Something about him scares me. Physically he could set her on fire, and she didn't know how she felt about that, either. You got no pain from a heart in the deep-freeze.

She didn't run up the stairs, because once she started running to him it would be hard to stop. So she went up slowly and sauntered into the living-room, where she could see him through the open door.

'Hard day?' he said.

'Busy, busy.'

'Take a chair.' She had been sitting for the last hour, but she sat and he said, 'I've got something for you.'

He put it in the palm of her hand—a Mizpah brooch—and the room swam around her. Her brooch, her great-grandmother's brooch. He had it. He had taken it. But between one breath and the next her mind cleared, because of course this was not the same brooch, and that she could have thought it might be even for a second appalled her, showing how she had let something that happened long ago warp her entire life. Because once, in somebody's power, it had been like the rape of her soul, and she had never been free. Ever since she had been a prisoner of her own cowardice, but that was over now and she looked up at him, her eyes brimming with sudden tears.

'Alice?' he said.

She blinked until her lashes were spiky. 'Thank you,' she said. 'This is so like that I might never have lost it. Where did you find it?'

In any good antique jeweller's shop. But he had searched it out for her, and she was filled with gratitude and the need to make amends. This was his second gift, and she had given nothing in return, not even trust.

'Let's take off,' she said.

'Now?'

'Tomorrow? I could manage the weekend.'

'I'd like that very much. Where shall we go?'

'Surprise me,' she said. 'Could that be arranged?'

'It could.'

'Any time after midday I could have a small bag packed.'

'I'll be waiting.'

She stood up, clutching her Mizpah brooch, and she knew he would take her in his arms, but this was not the time nor the place and she said, 'If I'm taking tomorrow afternoon off as well I should do a little more work tonight.'

He gestured wry resignation, then smiled at her, and she smiled back. 'Clients in the morning, but from midday I will concentrate entirely on you,' she said gaily.

'That's a promise?'

'I promise.' She was laughing, but she was promising herself in quiet earnest to put the memories behind her, to give without fear, to start from this day forward to *live* . . .

CHAPTER SIX

NEXT morning Alice woke excited and happy as a young girl in love for the first time.

She was a woman, and she was not in love, but everything seemed new and thrilling, and, showering and dressing, she let herself dream deliciously of the man who exuded a white-hot sensuality that would be all hers for this weekend at least.

She was not looking beyond that. She was taking what was offered here and now, making up for what should have been the carefree years. It amused her that she looked the same pale, cool blonde as yesterday, although it was hard to stop smiling as she packed her case.

The skies were still grey and the weather forecast was gloomy, so warm clothes were in order. She packed a cotton nightshirt that was her closest to glamour sleepwear—usually she wore men's pyjamas—and a black off-the-shoulder dress with her silk jacket, and she would travel in a suit and top coat, throwing a mac into the car boot. That should get her through two days, coming back Sunday. And two nights.

She felt vibrantly alive, and she could not believe how she had let herself brood all these years over a nightmare, something that had never happened in real life. One thing, she thought, I picked the right one to shock me awake. He operates well with earthquakes, as Owen French can testify.

She smiled at that, closed the lid of her case, and took coffee and toast to her desk. When Ivan passed the open office door, carrying a morning paper, he called, 'Twelve o'clock.'

'Rely on it,' she carolled back.

She was telling no one that she would be away. She would be home again before most of them found out, if they ever did. The answerphone would take messages, and she was not discussing this with anyone.

She met several folk this morning who had heard the Martin and Robin gossip, and she shrugged that off as a load of rubbish, and wondered how they would react if she'd said, But Ivan Blackmore and I are just off together for the weekend. I don't know where. He's booking us in somewhere. Of *course* a single room. I can't keep my hands off him and he says he feels the same about me.

All her tasks went smoothly. Everybody seemed to co-operate and she was through before midday. Driving down a road of good-sized detached houses set in largish gardens, she came to Patsy's home, and, on impulse, turned into the drive. She had time to spare; she would call on Granny Rosa.

She had always been fond of Patsy's grandmother, right from when her father would sometimes leave her with Patsy in Granny Rosa's van, drinking nettle pop, while he and the senior Perinnis talked business in the house.

She was 'young Alice' to Granny then and she was 'young Alice' now as she crossed the lawns and rounded the flowerbeds, to where the van had rested so long beside the beech hedge that the wheels had sunk well down in the turf, although Granny Rosa still talked as if she might be taking it on the open road again next week.

But inside crystal glassware sparkled, and the cupboards and shelves were filled with richly coloured Royal Doulton china. The bobbled curtains and upholstery were dark red velvet, and it was all clean as a new pin.

Granny was at home, studying racing form on the sports pages. 'Come in,' she called, and nodded when Alice opened the door. 'I've been expecting you, young Alice.'

Alice still called sometimes, but now she said, 'Have you?'

'It's that young man.'

In a way it was—Alice had him very much on her mind—but now she asked, 'Why do you think that?'

'I saw the way you looked at him.'

Not that often. Most of the time Alice had avoided looking at Ivan. Maybe Granny was psychic. Alice sat on the button-backed seat that ran along one side of the van and asked bluntly, 'Do you have second sight? Can you really tell what's going to happen?'

It wouldn't have surprised her if she had been ordered out, but instead Granny chuckled, 'Not with horses,' and Alice smiled. Her father could never resist backing Granny's tips, though most of them turned out to be also-rans.

Granny was treating this as a joke and so it surely was, because nobody could know the future. But when Granny Rosa said, 'No, thank the Lord,' it astonished Alice that she should be admitting being a phoney.

She had stopped smiling now. She looked and sounded serious. 'I've known them as has, and it's more of a curse than a blessing. What I've had, young Alice, and I've got 'em still, are sharp eyes. Most folk see no further than the end of their nose, but this man we're talking about, I knew as soon as I clapped eyes on him he wasn't for you.'

Alice said quietly, 'You were wrong, reading his hand. He had a tough start; he was reared in an orphanage.'

'Got away from it, didn't he?' said Granny.

'Well, yes.'

'I know a travelling man when I see one, and he's restless to the bone. Nobody'll hold him back; he'll be away before long. And you're a homemaker,' Granny went on. 'Always have been.'

'So I have,' said Alice.

She looked around her. 'Can I bring him to visit?' she asked. 'As a travelling man, he'd appreciate this.'

'He'd be welcome.' Granny's smile was roguish. 'I could have him hitching up and travelling with me.'

Alice laughed. 'You may be able to con most of the people most of the time,' she said, 'but I think you're a wicked woman.'

'Always have been,' said Granny Rosa smugly. 'Put something on Rob Roy in the two-thirty at Stratford tomorrow.'

'Hmm,' said Alice.

Ivan was waiting for her when she got back home, and she said, 'I've just come from Granny Rosa's.'

'Any messages?'

'She warned me against you again, because you have restless bones and I'm an old stick-in-the-mud. And she gave me a tip for the two-thirty tomorrow.'

'How is she as a tipster?'

'Awful; I shouldn't bother.'

It took her no time to collect her case. The phone was ringing, but she let it ring; there was no one she wanted to talk to. And, closing the front door behind her, she was almost sure they were being watched as Ivan carried her case to his car—by Karen Morton or some other neighbour, who would not know what to make of this.

She couldn't care less what they thought. When he turned to look at her, just before starting the engine, her heart started pounding and her fingers curled and tightened in her lap.

'Alice,' he said softly, gently touching her face, and her name on his lips sent her weak. He really was a most disturbing man.

'Yes?' Her voice was husky and her eyelashes felt heavy, so that she looked up at him slowly and languorously.

'You are very beautiful.' Today she was. She had never been quite sure before. 'And we are going to have a wonderful time,' he said.

She was already having a wonderful time, heading for where he was not telling her yet. Her spirits were sky-high and her heart was light as a balloon in a high wind. Sitting beside him, enjoying the closeness of his long, strong body, she was already having the time of her life.

Before long she was literally flying. When the road signs continued to indicate the airport she did say, 'Where are we going? I don't have my passport.'

'You don't need it,' he said, and nor did she, for Jersey—because it was a little Jersey plane she was guided to—and she settled down in a window seat, immeasurably more excited than she had been a few weeks before, flying out to Florida in a jumbo jet with Martin.

She was not the same woman and this was not the same man. That holiday had been enjoyable. She had looked forward to it and she had had a good time, but with Ivan everything was breathtaking.

Looking down on the sea, spotting the coastline through breaks in the clouds, was fresh and marvellous, as if she was seeing for the first time something she would never forget. And even the casual contact of his arm against her shoulder was more sensually stirring than Martin hugging her tight.

She thought, This isn't fancying a man. This is needing just this one, as if I have been starving for years, so that his lightest touch goes deep inside me, filling an emptiness.

There was a hired car waiting, and the girl handing it over seemed to feel she ought to recognise them. As they drove away Alice said, 'She's seen you on the back of a book; she was trying to remember you.'

'Not me,' he said. 'It was you. She couldn't make up her mind if you're a model or an actress, but she knew you had to be one or the other with your looks.'

Not true, but she tossed her hair back and laughed, 'Now where?'

The hotel looked like a French château, overlooking the bay of St Helier, and for its size it seemed strangely empty. The foyer was a great entrance hall, thickly carpeted, with a curving staircase leading up to a galleried floor, and a small avenue of well lit shops down a wide empty corridor.

Their room up on the third floor was palatial: two single beds as large as doubles, and white and gold Empire furniture that would have graced a château.

'Oh, my gosh,' said Alice, and then, '*Are* we all alone? How can they run a place this size without customers?'

Ivan was at the window. Below she could see the dome of a glass roof. 'They don't,' he said. 'It's a conference hotel, only there isn't a conference this week and the tourist season hasn't started.'

'If there should be a fire I hope they'll remember us.'

'They won't forget you,' he said.

'I've never been to Jersey before.' It wasn't shyness that made her change the subject. She had thought that as soon as they were alone she would be hurling herself into his arms, but now she was prolonging the waiting—not holding off exactly, but flirting a little.

'Shall we go sightseeing?' he said.

'Yes, please.'

They took in the hotel first, and that was an eye-opener, with a magnificent ballroom and a swimming-pool surrounded by the marble statues and pillars of a Roman baths. All deserted, except for staff flitting here and there. It was impressive, luxurious, and more than slightly eerie. But down a wide flight of steps and across a forecourt they came out into the streets of the island's capital and wandered like tourists.

Well, Alice did. She was a tourist, fascinated by the shops, the sights. And Ivan was humouring her, smiling at her enthusiasm. Sometimes she wondered at it herself, because she was acting out of character, but all the time excitement was churning in her. And when they went into a pretty little restaurant on the quayside she toyed with a kiwi, nectarine and straw-berry tart, and remembered how it sometimes was when she was a young child, before her birthday,

before Christmas, when looking forward to something intensely could trigger a sick headache.

It would be pathetic if she let that happen now she
was a grown, mature woman, too childish to contem-
plate, and she sipped her lemon tea and slowed down
her words and began to act her age.

In the hotel they walked down the 'street' of shops:
a jeweller's, two boutiques, a confectioner's, a newsagent's and bookshop. Alice bought a guidebook, Ivan
got the local newspapers, and when they reached a
lounge with phone booths he said, 'I should be making
a couple of calls.'

There was a phone in the bedroom but she said, 'I
should too. I'll phone upstairs and you ring here and
then we'll both be through,' and went to the lift and
ran along the corridor, slipping her plastic card into
the lock and leaving the door unlatched.

There were no calls she had to make, but she wanted
to get into the bathroom and changed, because now
she was jittery. It made no sense, but she didn't want
to strip in front of him. Not just yet. After dinner
and a few drinks it would be easier.

She moved at speed, and when he tapped on the
bathroom door she called, 'Nearly ready.' And she
was. She came out with hair smooth and her skin
flawless, wearing the off-the-shoulder black dress.

'You're a quick change,' he said.

'Yes.' She could feel the colour rising in her cheeks.
'And I'm ravenous; do you think the food's good?'

'So they say.'

The glass-domed roof was glowing from the
brightness below, and the lights of the town glittered
like diamonds in the dark sky. Looking out on the
lights, Alice told herself, I have never been so happy.

Granny Rosa is right: we are oil and water, he and I, and there is no future for us. But letting him love me will be the best thing that ever happened to me, and what comes after can never take that away.

She stayed where she was until he came up behind her, and when she turned he was so close that she could hardly breathe, much less speak.

'Did you get through?' he asked.

'What?'

'Your telephone calls.'

'Oh, that!' He'd known she couldn't have spent time on the telephone as well as in the bathroom. If he guessed that she had rushed ahead to get changed unobserved he would think she was such a ninny.

She managed a little shrug. 'Engaged; I'll try later.'

'You could try now.'

'Or I might not bother,' she said. 'Not for tonight, anyway. They were business calls; they'll wait. And I'm starving.'

He looked steadily at her for a moment, and she knew that if he touched her she was lost; then he smiled. 'I wouldn't keep a lady from her dinner.'

She nearly said, Who needs dinner? She nearly reached out to pull him against her. But the night was young and they would be coming back to this room together and this was part of the overture, leading up to their mutual seduction.

Heaven knew she wanted that, but she didn't want to miss any of the fun on the way, and after years of being cool and reserved she would enjoy teasing and tantalising, and carrying on like a sex bomb, for the next hour or two.

She went ahead out of the room, and just outside the door she slipped her hand through his arm and smiled up. 'You said your apartment and my room were too cluttered. Well, we've got space and privacy now for all sorts of energetic moves. If we decided on the ballroom we'd probably have it to ourselves.'

'It's a thought. With or without spotlights?'

'No spotlights, but muted lighting's OK.' They had reached the lifts and the staircase. They took the stairs, seeing nobody. 'Because you are beautiful,' she said, and he said,

'That's my line. You are beautiful; I look like a Mafia hit man.'

'That too,' she said.

The dining-room was under the glass-domed roof, like a huge Edwardian conservatory, with palms growing and spindly-trunked flowering trees set in big white tubs.

All but a small area was roped off, and their fellow diners looked like commercial travellers and off-season holiday-makers. Alice was aware of turning heads as they were shown to a table, and, whatever Ivan said, she knew that he held most of the glances—from the women in particular. Men usually gave her an admiring once-over, but women kept looking across at Ivan. Any time during the meal if she looked around she would catch somebody's eye. She could understand that, although she did find herself giving some chilly looks back.

She told herself that she wasn't being possessive, it was just an automatic reaction; and neither did she ask who he had been phoning, although she wondered. Besides, if he'd asked who she'd been phoning, she would have had to lie to him.

There was no possessiveness in this relationship, but there was a lovely intimacy, and her friends would have thought this was an alien Alice, with her flirtatious repartee and the blatant invitation of her body language.

This Alice touched across the table, leaned forward to whisper. So did he. If they had been a honeymoon couple they could not have been more wrapped up in each other. She had never known a closeness like it, where she was beginning to believe that she could be outrageous and downright silly, and he would still find her totally desirable.

She drank champagne and she ate rich food, and when she was faced with the sweets trolley she looked at a strawberry gâteau and remembered the kiwi, nectarine and strawberry tart, and began to feel queasy again.

She stopped eating at that stage and she had no more wine, and when she touched her cheeks with her fingertips she could feel how flushed her face was. His face wasn't flushed. His tanned skin looked cool, and his hands were steady, while hers had the shakes.

He wanted her. He had been telling her so by word and touch all the way through their meal. That was intoxicating enough to make her head spin, and by now she was so dazzled that it was like stardust in front of her eyes, a glittering in the air.

She drank coffee, and cigarette smoke from another table was making her eyes burn, and a pulse was beginning to pound in her left temple.

'Shall we go up?' he said.

Out of the dining-room the throbbing was getting worse, so that climbing the stairs seemed too much of an effort and she turned almost blindly for the lift. Ivan held her as she leaned against the side of the lift, asking anxiously, 'What is it?'

'I don't feel so good.' She could hardly see his face now for the flashing lights, and the pounding pain was as if she was in for a migraine attack.

She had had migraines before; stress could cause them. This could be a fit of the vapours like that of a Victorian bride, and she had to lie down, take some pain-killers, and it would pass.

'It's a headache,' she said, and Ivan drawled,

'That's original,' and at once, 'Sorry.' He supported her as she walked slowly to their door, and she lay on her bed, one hand shielding her tender eye and throbbing temple from the light.

She heard him lifting the phone and whispered, 'What are you doing?'

'Getting a doctor.'

'I don't need a doctor. It's just a headache. I know; I get them sometimes. I just need some pain-killers.'

He put down the phone again and she closed her eyes, and then he was laying a cold wet compress on her forehead and telling her, 'I'll be right back.'

Maybe this wouldn't develop into a full-blown migraine. They didn't usually strike so suddenly, with no real warning except for the 'firework display', but it was already blinding her, and her only hope was to keep very still and very quiet, because if she moved she could be very sick.

She swallowed the pills he brought her, coughing at the trickle of water going down her throat, and even coughing hurt. 'Sorry,' she whispered. 'I'm so sorry.'

'Let's get you into bed,' he said.

She wasn't wearing much and he undressed her gently and deftly, so that she hardly had to move at all while her clothes slipped off. She thought, You must have had practice, and felt more dead than alive as he put her between the sheets and she turned her burning face into the cool cotton pillowcase.

The pills were effective, dulling the savage stabbing until she was breathing more easily and drowsiness was creeping over her. A soporific would be the best medicine of all. Sleep helped recovery like nothing else, and as she sank deeper into the comforting dark she thought, In a little while I shall feel better and then I will go over to his bed.

When she woke the room was dark, with just enough light from the window for her to see the shape in the other bed, and she raised her head cautiously from the pillow. She thought he was asleep. There was no sound from him at all. But as she lay down again he asked, 'How are you?'

A pulse, still beating faintly in her temples, reminded her that she was not yet cured. 'It's still there, but it's getting better.'

'Anything you want?'

'No, I'll be fine in the morning.'

'That's a promise?' Her promises were becoming a joke, but he sounded as if he was smiling, and she promised fervently, '*Yes.*'

'Then go to sleep till morning,' he said, and that was what she must do to see this wretched headache well and truly off, although what she would have liked to do was for him to come to her and hold her gently, so that she could have gone back to sleep in his arms.

When she woke again she blinked in the daylight and moved her head very slightly at first. Nothing hurt, and she breathed deeply and thankfully, like a swimmer coming up from the depths.

Sometimes a headache did last into the next day, but not this one, and she sat up, letting the sheet slip from her bare shoulders. Ivan's bed was empty and she called, 'Where are you?'

He came out of the bathroom, a towel fastened round his waist, asking, 'How are you?'

'It's a miracle.' And she hugged herself, beaming. It always felt that way. Whoever it was who had said that a devastating headache was next door to dying had been there.

Ivan sat on the side of her bed, looking hard at her. 'Do you get many headaches?'

She was glad he was concerned, but there was no need, because she didn't. She said, 'Just the occasional killer, and they're common enough. Seventy per cent of the population get them. There's a bit of useless information for you. I blame the champagne.'

'You take it easy.'

He put a hand on her forehead, and there was no fever there, although she must be sticky from last night's sweat and the residue of make-up. 'Can I have the bathroom?' she asked.

'It's all yours.'

She pushed back the bedclothes and set her feet on the carpet. She was not surprised to find that all she had on was a skimpy pair of knickers. Her legs were long and slender, and her body was taut, stomach flat, waist small, breasts firm; but Ivan was still looking at her more like a doctor than a lover, and he put a hand to steady her, asking, 'Can you manage?'

'Of course.' She hadn't wobbled at all until he touched her. 'When they're over they're over,' she said, and saw herself in the dressing-table mirror.

The body was fine, but the face was a mess, with mascara streaked down her cheeks and her hair straggling over her eyes. She held the edge of the table and gaped at her reflection. 'Don't look,' she said. 'I look like the Bride of Frankenstein.'

'Well, Frankenstein can't have you,' he said, and she laughed and went into the bathroom, sponging herself down and removing every scrap of stale make-up.

She felt fresher and cleaner after that, although with her natural pallor she always looked less healthy than she was. She had heard the knock on the door, and when she came out of the bathroom she saw that breakfast had been brought up. There was a tray on the table by the window.

'Coffee?' he said.

He was dressed, in grey trousers, grey jacket and black roll-necked sweater. She was still wearing her towelling robe, and she would have liked to sit at the dressing-table, put some colour into her face, and brush her hair. But the coffee was poured, and she needed it.

It was a continental breakfast, with orange juice and hot croissants. 'Is this all right?' he asked her. 'I didn't think you'd be wanting cooked food.'

She always ate a light breakfast, and she could have reassured him that she didn't need cosseting because there was nothing the matter with her. But it was comforting to know that he was concerned.

She said, 'By lunchtime I'll have a healthy appetite, but no more champagne,' and they sat over breakfast for half an hour or so, looking through the local papers he had brought up last night, reading bits out to each other.

When a crumb stuck in Alice's throat and she coughed to clear it Ivan asked, 'Are you all right?'

She had let him pour coffee, and butter croissants—do everything for her, short of feeding her. Her men had always been ready to fuss around, but with him it was different. Because he was so tough, tenderness from him was unexpected and touching, and she thought, I could love you—not just make love, but love you with all my heart—and then you would go away and I would be left behind. I could love you deeply, but I must not.

She said, 'I'm fine. It was just a headache and it's gone. I'm naturally pasty-faced; you know that. I'm not sick.'

'Don't be,' he said.

He got up and she stood up to meet him and he put his arms around her, under the robe, against her smooth, warm skin. She could feel the urgency inside her, the hunger aching to be filled, but when he kissed her she went rigid.

Then she heard herself ask, 'Where are we going today?'

The words jerked out when she should have kept quiet, and he said, 'Where's the guidebook?' and she was picking it up from her bedside table and giving it to him.

After that she dressed and brushed her hair and put on some make-up while he sat down again, reading out from the guidebook. There were beaches of golden sands and expanses of wild heathland, and she spoke through stiff lips as she applied lipstick. 'Would you mind if we went for the beaches rather than the gorse and heather?'

'You don't need to choose,' he said. 'The island's only twelve miles by six. You can have it all.'

She turned on her stool. 'Funny you should say that. Today I think I can.' There was nothing else she wanted but to be with him and she had that. He closed the book and smiled at her.

'So you shall,' he said.

It was a day that seemed to have everything. There was hardly any traffic on the roads. They drove along in what could have been a world of their own and, when they parked, theirs was the only car on a hill overlooking a magnificent sweep of smooth shining sands.

They took the footpath down and crossed the sand to the water's edge, where the surf came crashing in. The air was salty and cold, but in no time she was warm as she walked, sometimes with Ivan's arm around her shoulders, sometimes hand in hand. Always linked. Not always talking. More often, so far as Alice was concerned, just revelling in being together and hardly needing words.

In the summer the sea and the shore would be crowded, and she could imagine the sun on her face now as a glow of health and happiness pervaded her.

'I could swim here,' she said, and she almost felt that she could strip off and dive in. 'Do you swim?'

'Yes. But not here, today.'

'It's lovely, though, isn't it?'

Atlantic rollers were sweeping in and spumes of spray showed rocks beneath the surface, and Ivan laughed. 'This isn't a Florida swimming-pool, young Alice.'

He had heard Granny Rosa call her that, and the Florida swimming-pool was a sure guess. She remem-

bered swimming a leisurely backstroke in the
Roystons' pool, hardly getting her face wet, while
Martin ploughed along beside her saying, 'All right,
all right,' as she explained yet again that she was not
a marrying woman.

That was a situation that would never arise with
Ivan, and of course that was how she wanted it, and
she looked from the sea to the sands, seized with a
restlessness that made her start running. Up to now
they had only been strolling, but the sand was hard
and firm, and in spite of her winter coat and sturdy
shoes the running was easy. And exhilarating. The
man kept pace beside her, and no way could she
outpace him, but, like playing a game of tag, she
dodged and darted, with all the wide deserted beach
as a playground.

She was laughing and so was he, and she twirled
like a dancer, evading him a couple of times and racing
all out until finally he caught her and she couldn't
squirm out of his grip and ended laughing, her face
pressed against him then throwing her head back, and
he had stopped smiling, and what she saw in his eyes
was unreadable.

'Shall we?' he said. 'Here and now?'

They must have been tiny figures in an empty land-
scape, but he had to be joking, and she said, 'How
do we know there aren't half a dozen bird watchers
with power-zoom binoculars trained on us?'

He smiled again. 'An over-active imagination; that's
your trouble.' And arm in arm they began to walk
back towards the car.

It was high tide at Devil's Hole, with the sea pouring
into a huge crevice in the rocks, and producing a

roaring that was down in the guidebook as the devil calling to lost souls.

They were all the audience the devil had today, and after listening, and marvelling because it was impressive—both the noise and the spectacle of the sea foaming out in great white waves—Alice said, 'Well, I'm not answering him; how about you?'

'I'm not lost; I know where I'm going.'

She laughed—it was a day for laughter—and asked, 'Where are you going?'

'To get some food,' he said. 'I'm not having you with another headache from malnutrition.'

She was hungry. It was well into lunchtime, and they found an old granite farmhouse that sold superb farmhouse fare. There was only one other couple in the dining-room, and Alice thought, I'd like to stay here, to sleep in a little room under the eaves and maybe take out a boat and sail over the sea to France.

She could imagine that. Today she could have had a dozen different holidays, all with Ivan; they had crammed so much into a few short hours. And driving back to the hotel, when the light had faded and night was falling, she smiled at the thought of the quiet evening ahead and the quiet room waiting for them.

The forecourt car park was full. There had been plenty of spaces up to now, but tonight they were hard pressed to find one, and for the first time the foyer was crowded.

Of course it was Saturday night and obviously there was a function of some sort, and they went up the stairs, looking down on the colourful throng below. 'I was beginning to worry about this place,' said Alice. 'It's reassuring to see some more customers besides us.'

'I could have done without them. Shall we have dinner in our room?'

'That would be nice.'

There was a white envelope propped up against the mirror of the dressing-table, and she waited while he opened it. Then he said, 'It's Valentine's Day.'

'So?' She knew that. Some of her clients had used the Valentine's Day theme in adverts.

He handed her the letter on hotel paper, inviting them, as resident guests for the weekend, to the Valentine's Day banquet and ball.

'"At no extra cost",' she read out and laughed. 'How about that? And I was the one who said there was no such thing as a free freebie.'

'What do we do?'

'Can you dance?'

'About on a par with Granny Rosa's fortune-telling. More miss than hit.'

She looked down. 'I hope so, with your size feet. But I'm a lively mover, so we could chance it.'

'Why not?'

This was a bonus, ending the day with a party, so she didn't admit that she would rather they stayed on their own. 'Then I'd better get changed,' she said.

It was the little black dress again, this time with the silk jacket. She knew that she looked good, and he was stunning in a superbly cut suit, grey silk shirt and tie. He had to be about six feet four, and it was silly but she wanted to show him off. She didn't know a soul here, but she would enjoy walking in with him.

'What's wrong?' he said, and she had been giving him a speculative look.

'Not a thing.' She ran the tip of her tongue between her lips, her eyes dancing. 'I was thinking that any girl would be proud to be seen with you.'

'You're a flatterer. It's all that public relations blarney you're always handing out.'

'Cross my heart.' She did, tracing a cross like a child, and he put a hand over her fingers against her breast, and she laughed, because her heart had to be thudding loud enough to be heard, and if they were going to join the revellers they had to go now.

For the first time they met other guests in the corridor, waiting for the lifts and walking down the stairs. There was no roped-off area in the dining-room tonight. Every table was set and most of the places were taken.

Alice and Ivan were seated with a couple who were halfway through their meal and more than halfway through a bottle of pink champagne. They greeted the newcomers like old friends, and in no time the woman was telling Alice that they lived locally and always came to the Valentine Ball because they had got engaged here five years ago.

She looked at Alice's ringless hand and then at Ivan and giggled and wished Alice good luck.

'Thank you,' Alice said demurely, giving Ivan a mischievous sideways glance. She had all the luck she needed tonight and she was glad they had come down, because this was fun and any time at all she could say, 'Shall we go?' and they could be alone together.

The heart motif was everywhere, from the posies of tiny flowers that were the centrepiece of every table, to the croutons in the soup and the silver heart-shaped balloons bobbing high above under the glass roof.

The food was food for sweethearts: poached salmon with caviare, and an iced concoction with passion-fruit and raspberry sauce; and from the ballroom—wide doors had been opened, connecting it with the dining-room—the music was love-songs with a dreamy tempo.

As the dining-room emptied the ballroom filled, and Alice and Ivan were among the last to leave their table. Before they did there was the little ritual of the silver balloon. Balloons had been continually floating up, and this, the couple at their table informed them, was tradition.

You wrote your name and table number on the small hotel-headed label attached, then your balloon joined the others, and at the end of the evening windows opened up there and they were wafted off into the night. There were prizes for the ones picked up furthest away by the closing date, midnight next Saturday.

As she let her balloon go this year the woman at their table told them that the year before last she had won a prize—a big teddy bear, which their little girl loved.

As Alice wrote 'Ivan and Alice, No. 36' and let the string slide through her fingers she said, 'That's the second balloon to get away from me in less than a week.'

'More fool them,' Ivan said. 'Who'd want to get away from you?' And the waiter who had brought the balloon over looked as if he agreed.

The ballroom glittered with chandeliers, and the floor was a shifting pattern of colour as the dancers moved with the music. There were seats and small tables around, and they sat with a bottle of wine, listening to the 'Anniversary Waltz', a request, being sung by a girl with a pleasantly husky voice.

'Probably our pair,' said Alice. Most of those here tonight would have a special song. Lovers did, the romantic ones who celebrated Valentine's Day. This could be her song, because she was listening to it now with Ivan, although he would have forgotten that by morning.

A waitress was offering them a bowl of what looked like puffy pink and blue wafer biscuits, and Alice said, 'No, thanks.'

'You don't eat them,' the waitress said. 'You pop 'em; they've got sort of mottoes inside.'

So Alice took a couple and handed one to Ivan. The rice paper of hers crumbled, spilling out a tiny scrap of paper. She smoothed it out and read, '"Princess Charming will soon be entering your life". Will she now?'

'Probably a client,' he said. 'Aiming for showbiz.'

She had a blue biscuit and so did he. She should have realised they were colour-sexed. 'What does yours say?' she asked.

He read, '"You should trust the one you love".'

Love was all around them—this was love's festival—but the word had never been spoken between them and she couldn't lay claim to it. She said, 'You can have Princess Charming if you like.'

'I don't,' he said. 'I'm not a believer in fairy-tales.'

A young man was suddenly beside Alice—an eager young man with flopping hair and bright eyes. 'Would you like . . . ?' he began, and Ivan looked round and at him.

The light was on Alice. She had slung the jacket over the back of her chair, and light was shining on her smooth hair and on her bare white shoulders. Her face was pale and almost perfect.

Ivan had been sitting with his back to the dancers, but when he leaned forward the young man took a step back. Then he answered himself, 'No, you wouldn't,' and went off to try his luck elsewhere.

'You do have a way with you,' said Alice. 'Like a male Medusa. You turn them to stone.'

'Did you want to dance with him?'

'No. Will you dance with me?'

'Any time.'

This was a big ballroom, the floor was not crowded, and the Valentine Ball was no disco. Dancers danced with their arms around their partners, and Alice laced her fingers behind his head and stood for a moment in the circle of his arms.

She knew they would dance easily together because they were in tune with each other, and this was as natural as walking across the sands holding hands. Except that music was playing here and they were not alone.

But they could have been alone. When she closed her eyes they could have been dancing in an empty ballroom, and the light baritone voice singing 'Greensleeves' could have been in her mind.

She smiled up at Ivan. 'Now this is real old-time music.'

'They don't come much older,' he said, and she let her head droop on his shoulder and felt his lips in her hair. There was such security in his nearness, as if his strength was her protection.

'Greensleeves was all my joy, Greensleeves was my delight,' the singer sang, and she thought, Yes, he is my joy and my delight, because I am crazy for him.

'Greensleeves was my heart of gold...' Her lips curved; she was not so sure about the heart of gold. That made her smile, and she looked up again, and met dark eyes in an unsmiling face.

'Let's get out of here,' he said harshly.

She nodded and he caught her wrist and they threaded their way through the dancers. She grabbed her jacket—she had almost forgotten it—and it seemed to her that the crowds melted away. There was quite a crowd—the bar was full, and so was the foyer—and they passed several guests on the stairs.

Some must be staying the night, and she wondered if they were all lovers. She hardly saw them clearly. Her heart was racing and her blood was on fire. She was burning up for him. While he opened the door of their room she held on to his arm, her fingers clutching his sleeve, and inside the room he kissed her, lifting her off her feet, kissed her and kissed her, and she was kissing him back as he held her tight and tighter until she was almost fainting.

She had dropped her coat and kicked off her shoes, and her dress—all that she was wearing—had fallen away, and he picked her up naked and put her on a bed.

Light came through the window, and it was enough. She watched him starting to strip, the broad shoulders with their rippling muscles tapering down to a narrow waist, his face in shadow. A powerful man, dangerous and lithe as a tiger.

Her head was pounding again, not with pain this time, although she put fingers up to her temples, then stretched her arms above her head. Her wrists brushed the bedhead and she was caught, transfixed, unable

to move, back in her old room with the man at the
window, as helpless as if cords held her.

A half-scream burst from her. 'No...' And as he
came towards her she gasped, 'Don't touch me.'

She had to be going mad. She knew where she was,
who he was, but the terror was real. The past was
superimposed on the present, and she was choking as
though a gag were suffocating her.

Lights went on blindingly and she covered her face,
cowering. He was beside her now, and she couldn't
look at him. She had to hold herself together, she had
to explain, but when she did look for him he was
dressed. 'Count me out,' he said. 'I'm playing no more
of these games.'

And the door closed behind him as she whimpered,
'Wait.'

She staggered from the bed to the door and had
the door open, but he was at the end of the corridor
and she was naked, and when she looked for her
clothes, scattered around on the floor, she was shaking
so badly that she could hardly pick them up, let alone
get into them.

In the bathroom she threw cold water in her face
and huddled into her bathrobe, and sat on the edge
of a bed, rocking backwards and forwards.

She *was* going insane. This had never happened to
her before, so why had it happened with the only man
she had ever really wanted? If she had given herself
to him it would have been with no reservations.

With Ivan she would have had no defences left; and
that was why she was afraid. More than afraid. She
was terrified, because buried deep in her subconscious, even though her conscious mind had rejected
it, was still the dread of any man having so much

power over her. That was why she had delayed total
surrender in a dozen different ways, and, when the
moment of naked truth finally came, it had blown her
mind.

She dressed, although she was still shaking, but in
the open doorway she was lost again, because she had
no idea where to find him. Not back with the dancers,
she knew. Nor, she thought, in the bar. Outside somewhere. But if she wandered the streets searching, the
odds of finding him were slight. He would come back
here some time. She would have to wait here.

She went to the window, and sat huddled in a chair
as the music played love-songs below, facing the im-
possibility of ever putting things right, because what
could she say to him?

I have this problem. It's never been this bad before.
Only with you because you are the only one who
could have taken my body and my soul. And you are
the only one who reminded me of a rapist I used
to know...

CHAPTER SEVEN

ALICE was still sitting alone at the window when the silver balloons soared up into the sky at the end of the Valentine Ball. A chorus of cheers and laughter followed them and her eyes brimmed with tears, blurring the bobbing balloons into a floating silver skein.

Ours should be a non-starter, she thought, landing on the first roof, stuck in the guttering. She tried to smile and felt pathetic, sitting here with trembling lips and brimming eyes. Such a fool, such a stupid idiot of a woman.

She had been waiting for hours, and it felt like it. When she stood up she was stiff, because she had sat tense and unmoving. Perhaps he wasn't coming back tonight. He could easily find himself another bed; off season the town must be full of them. And someone to share it if he was that frustrated.

Somehow she couldn't imagine him with a casual pick-up, but she didn't know. And there was nothing she could do about anything, so she might as well get into bed herself.

She undressed again, putting her clothes neatly aside this time, and washed and cleaned her teeth, all the time feeling punch-drunk. She had switched off the main light, but she left a bedside lamp on and sat up in bed for a while, hands looped round her ankles, head bowed on her knees.

Her mind was whirling. What could she say? What could she do? She had a small, crazy hope that when she saw him again the right words would come, but the longer he was away, the fainter that hope became.

She lay down at last, the pillows piled up behind her, and when she closed her eyes images danced in her head. Clearly, in every detail, she saw again her old room, and the man in the Balaclava, who had been nothing like Ivan, not nearly as tall. But she remembered the terror still and thought that she always would, and tried to shut it away.

With her mind in turmoil there was no question of sleep. The Valentine party was over—she had heard some of the revellers going to their rooms along the corridor—and for a long time there was near silence, broken by the sound of an occasional car, a dog barking, a phone ringing faintly.

She watched the minutes and the hours tick by on her small travelling clock, like life-blood draining away, and just before three she heard the lock on the bedroom door click back.

She was sitting upright when he stepped into the room, and her voice came out high and not quite steady. 'I want to talk; I want to explain.'

'There's nothing to explain. It's your right to say no and you said it.' He didn't sound resentful. He sounded like somebody being pestered by a pushy child, holding them off and smiling down at them. 'Let's leave it at that,' he said, and went into the bathroom, leaving her speechless.

She didn't know how she would have explained, but she had been hoping against hope that if he would put his arms around her she might be able to stammer

something. Well, he hadn't, and nor would he; she
was pretty sure of that.

She sat up in her bed, her own arms wrapped
around her, and from the bathroom she could hear
the shower swishing down. She 'saw' his broad
shoulders again, the smooth, hard-muscled back,
water cascading over him and turning the dark hair
into a thick, shining pelt.

He *was* beautiful. He was a stunningly sexy man
and she ached for him, and if he wouldn't listen to
words maybe actions would speak louder.

He didn't hear her push the bathroom door open.
The water was on full blast, streaming over his up-
turned face. She stepped under the flow, facing him,
her cotton nightshirt drenched and clinging to her.
'Hello,' she said.

He had wanted her, he had told her that, and she
couldn't get closer, and this had to make him laugh.
He did laugh—not long and not loud, but he
laughed—and reached up to turn off the water. Then
he stepped out and picked up a couple of towels,
handed one to her, and began to rub himself down
with the other.

'Very tempting,' he said, and she hadn't realised
how cold the water was until she began to shiver. 'But
you're not that beautiful.'

He left her in the bathroom, and she towelled herself
almost dry and hated him. And herself, so badly that
she could have rubbed her skin raw. He'd had his own
back there. Rejection for rejection, with macho pride
restored.

She didn't feel beautiful. She shrivelled inside, because she had never felt so ugly. She didn't think she
could face him again, and she almost considered

stretching out on the tiled floor among the thick fluffy towels rather than following him into the bedroom.

But of course she must get into her own bed. She didn't have to look at him nor speak to him. She turned the drier on to her hair for a few minutes, then came out of the bathroom wearing a towel.

She dropped the towel when she slid between the sheets, still damp enough to stick to them in places, and only looked towards him through narrowed eyes from under the duvet.

The lamp was out and he was in bed, turned away from her, but she could see the dark, wet hair, a shoulder and an arm, and she thought incredulously, He's either asleep or well on the way.

She should be asleep soon. It was after three, and she had to be tired after a day like this. Ahead was the flight home together—and how she was going to get through that she did not know—and she must get some sleep.

But she was taut with tension from head to foot, her nerves stretched to breaking-point. She tried to imagine herself somewhere else, anywhere, alone or with anybody else, but there was no escape through her imagination when she was aware of his nearness in every cell in her body.

If this stress didn't lead to a migraine nothing ever would again, and she couldn't plead a second headache. She'd get no sympathy next time; he'd take the plane and leave her here. She had to keep calm. She had to try to sleep.

Breathe deep and slow; that was the basic relaxation exercise. And she did that, and she could hear his deep, slow breathing. But he wasn't trying to relax.

He, damn him, was sleeping soundly, and she wanted
to throw the clock at him.

Another thing she could lose with him. Her temper.
She couldn't remember ever flying into a rage. She
must have had childish tantrums, but she had always
had to be older than her years; she had always
screamed silently.

It would have been a wonderful relief to bound over
there and hammer her fists into him and yell, Why
won't you listen to me? Why won't you help me? How
can you sleep when I'm screaming?

That she could imagine. She played that out in her
mind, although she never got as far as his reaction.
All the action was on her part, all kicking and
screaming, and she thought, I mustn't fall asleep
screaming. If I have a nightmare, he'll think it's
another trick.

But her dreams were quiet nightmares in which she
was running and stumbling down empty, endless
streets. She woke several times, remembered where she
was, remembered everything, and tossed and turned
before she drifted back into her lonely dreams.

She passed a wretchedly restless night, but she must
have been deeply asleep when the knock on the door
roused her, because she had to struggle awake, coming
up from under the bedclothes and looking blearily
around.

The sight of Ivan carrying a breakfast tray towards
the window table cleared her vision. The last time she
had looked at the clock it had been just before seven.
She had resolved to get up at seven, but it was after
eight now, and he was fully dressed and she was naked
between crumpled sheets.

She was out of bed and into the bathroom as he set down the tray, and she scrambled into clothes, and grabbed her make-up from the dressing-table, and took that into the bathroom for privacy.

He was drinking coffee, reading a paper, when she finally went over to the table. 'Good morning,' he said.

'Morning.' She poured coffee into the empty cup, sat down, and sipped a little. Then she said, 'I made a fool of myself last night.'

Anyone would agree with that. She agreed with it herself. He had been brutal, but she had been a fool. Now he looked at her with those piercing eyes and she looked for the butter. She didn't want it, but she didn't want to look at him either.

'How old are you?' he asked.

'Twenty-two; didn't you know?'

'I suppose I did, and you don't look sixteen any more than you look like a bashful virgin.' She couldn't deny that was how she had acted. 'You're neither, of course,' he said, 'and you do get your kicks out of stringing them alone and then kicking them in the teeth; I've seen that. I should have seen it coming my way; the signs were clear enough. You could have auditioned for RADA with that headache; it had me worried.'

'I wasn't...' she began. She had not been faking the savage pain, but it had been a delaying tactic, although she hadn't realised that at the time, and she finished wearily, 'Oh, forget it.'

'I don't think so. You're a knock-out for looks— you know that, of course—but sexually you're becoming a bore.'

Because she was so mixed up she hadn't played fair, and she said quietly, 'Please don't be angry.'

'I'm not angry.' The drawling voice was wry. 'I'd have enjoyed having you, but knowing I didn't and I won't doesn't worry me unduly.' She sat very still. 'But from now on don't waste your histrionics on me,' he said. 'And a word of advice. Don't go this far again, because you were taking one hell of a risk. Forced entry isn't my line, but you're going to get it soon if you carry on this way.'

She felt her face go white and cold, and he said, 'Don't look so mournful; the weekend wasn't wasted.' He sounded almost amused, telling her, 'It's been a pleasure having you around. You're a bright and funny lady, as well as being unfailingly decorative.'

That was the pat on the head after the blows to the face. Nothing mattered to him, because he didn't care. She cared too much; that was why she had panicked last night and why she would rather have had him angry this morning than cynically tolerant.

So what happened next? There were hours to get through before the plane went, and she asked, 'What do we do now? It isn't late.'

He raised an eyebrow in mock-surprise. 'You're not suggesting we jump into the sack?'

Of course she wasn't. He knew that. She muttered, 'I wasn't suggesting anything.'

'No? You're usually so good at suggestions.'

She had been: suggestions, promises, like a teasing teenager. Well, he was teasing her now. Young Alice, nearly twenty-three, going on sixteen.

'I'm meeting friends this morning,' he said. 'You could come along, but...' He let the word hang in the air, meaning he didn't think they would want her and neither did he; and she had some tatters of pride left.

She said, 'There are still places I want to see.'

'Do you need the car?'

'No.' She had no idea where she was going, but she would probably be walking.

'Then I'll take the cases, and see you at the airport about one o'clock.'

His case was packed and strapped down. He must have moved quietly in the short time she was sleeping heavily.

She left the toast she had buttered, and carried her coffee to the table by her bed while she took clothes from the wardrobe. But she didn't drink any more coffee; she concentrated on packing as quickly as possible. A weekend case didn't take long to fill, although she had to stop herself ramming in the contents anyhow, wet nightshirt and all, and pretend she was being methodical about it.

There were overnighters in the corridor and several waiting by the lifts. They took the stairs again and somebody said, 'Hello,' coming up as they went down. It was the anniversary pair who had shared their table, and Alice smiled back at them and Ivan said, 'Good morning.'

'Lovely, wasn't it?' said the woman, and whispered to Alice, 'We saw you leaving early.'

A hot blush rose in Alice's pale cheeks, delighting the woman, who said happily, 'See you again next year?'

'Who knows,' said Ivan. I know, thought Alice. As they went on down the stairs he said, 'There goes your Princess Charming; she seems to believe in fairy-tales.'

A girl at the reception desk leaned forward to smile at them. At Ivan, Alice noticed, and wondered what would happen if she walked over to the desk herself and said, Forget how it looks; he's still up for grabs.

She followed him through the wide doors, down the stone steps and round the hotel to where they had parked their car last night, and as he opened the boot to stack in the cases she asked, 'Have you settled?'

'Of course.'

'I want to pay my share.'

He closed the boot and got into the driving seat. 'I know,' he said. 'You don't owe anyone. Don't worry; you don't. I've paid more for less.' And somehow that seemed nearer an insult than a compliment.

She watched the car manoeuvring through the vehicles that were streaming out of the car park, and followed it into the streets. But he turned out of town and was out of sight while she stood on the pavement.

If he had said, Come along? she might have done. She had no plans, and she was curious about his friends. Perhaps he had gone round to them last night, or this might have been an earlier arrangement, but they would have been interesting, because he had no time for fools.

She would have behaved herself; she wouldn't have embarrassed him. Offhand she couldn't think of anything that would. Last night hadn't. She had been racked with guilt and seared by rejection, but he had slept well and woken prepared to shrug the whole thing off.

That was civilised. The idea of their being lovers had been a disaster, but maybe they could carry on as a couple who liked each other well enough.

Being alone had never bothered her before, but this morning she was at a loss. Perhaps it was because she had walked the same streets with Ivan, talking and laughing, her hand linked in his, that she was missing him every step of the way.

The shops were shut today; she couldn't wander around them. Nor could she spend, and that was as well, because she could have been tempted into mad extravagance, buying things she couldn't afford to cheer herself up.

She couldn't even take presents back, without everyone knowing where she had been and asking countless questions. Martin would be hurt and horrified, although he would probably forgive her if she explained that it had been a mistake and stopped on the brink of consummation. Nobody else would believe she hadn't been sleeping with Ivan Blackmore, but Martin would try very hard to believe her. And she knew she would tell him nothing, because right now she could hardly remember his name.

She walked aimlessly, killing time, none of the glances she got registering. For hours she sat in the harbour, watching the boats. The sea air should have been invigorating, but she still felt only half awake.

She wanted to go home. The flight and the drive might be awkward, with a man she had stripped naked for last night and then screamed, 'Don't touch me.' But when she called a taxi and said, 'To the airport,' and settled back in her seat she started to feel livelier.

Even sparring was better than being on her own. He could make cracks, he could call her young Alice as if she were an immature brat, but just being on her way to join him again was cheering her up.

His friends had come to see him off—a bearded scholarly-looking man and a well dressed woman. She had thought they might, and as soon as she spotted him she drew back, trying to keep out of sight but watching avidly.

The woman's dark red hair was immaculate in a French pleat, and her fuchsia and black suit was designer class. Ivan had his back to Alice, but the trio were obviously on very good terms, and when the woman put a hand on his arm it looked like a gesture she had made many times before. The bearded man was smiling and nodding, and Alice was sure they were saying, Don't leave it so long next time, and stay longer.

A girl passed her, running, making for the threesome. She was wearing jodhpurs and a bright yellow turtle-neck sweater, and her red hair was flame-bright, falling loose on her shoulders. She was a younger, prettier edition of the woman, and she threw herself into Ivan's arms, her excited squeal reaching Alice. 'I thought I was going to miss you; I never thought I'd get here in time.'

Jealousy knifed Alice, and Ivan looked across from hugging the girl and met her eyes. She almost turned away, but, having seen her, he obviously expected her to join them. He said something, and all their heads turned towards her. When she reached them the girl was still hanging on to him and the middle-aged couple were looking intrigued.

The girl was looking worried, and Alice knew she had a crush on Ivan Blackmore. More than a crush, maybe; she was no child, at nineteen or twenty.

He was introducing her. 'Alice Ashby, John, Diane and Liza Le Breton.' Hands were shaken and smiles exchanged, and Liza was waiting to hear what Alice was doing here. He might have told her parents, I'm meeting someone at the airport, but this seemed to be the first Liza had heard of her, and Alice said, 'I'm in PR.'

That sounded as professional as secretary or researcher, and could be platonic, although Liza said, 'I wouldn't have thought Ivan needed publicity.'

'Oh, Alice is invaluable; she comes up with some fantastic ideas.' He was laughing at her, and she wished she had said nothing. 'And how's life at the riding school?' he asked Liza.

She talked to Ivan while her parents listened fondly. Alice gathered that she worked at a riding school on the other side of the island, and this morning her mother had phoned and left a message that Ivan was here, leaving from the airport on a scheduled flight.

Liza had been out, exercising the horses, and when she had got back she was almost too late. She had jumped into a car and broken all speed records, and Alice thought sourly, I wonder she didn't stay on the horse and gallop over. Because she could imagine her on horseback, red hair flying.

She could imagine her riding over the downs with Ivan—he'd be at home on a horse, too—and Alice, who had never been on one in her life, felt that he had galloped away from her with these friends of his, while she stood on the sidelines, getting smaller and smaller until she was out of sight.

When they said goodbyes Diane said it had been nice meeting her and smiled as though she meant it, but Liza's eyes never left Ivan. He shook hands with John and kissed Diane and Liza on the cheek, and

Liza clung to him again, and Alice turned away because she did not want to see this.

As they handed in their cases she said, 'They're charming.'

'Yes,' he agreed.

As the plane was taxiing along the runway for take-off she asked, 'How long have you known the Le Bretons?'

'Quite a while.'

'Liza has a crush on you,' she said, smiling.

'I'm the wicked uncle; that's my attraction.'

'Are you her uncle?'

'Lord, no. John's an archaeologist; I met him on a dig. I've been to their home; we've kept in touch.'

'And you're a travelling man. Do you have friends all over the world?' It was better to keep him talking than to sit silently beside him. Small talk gave the illusion that she was at ease.

'I don't know about friends,' he said. 'I've got some far-flung contacts, if that will do.'

'And you keep in touch. That's friendly. When your lease is up, will you keep in touch with me?' She shouldn't have asked that. He gave her the amused glance that meant, Stop flirting. But she hadn't been.

'Why?' he said. 'Are you looking for a wicked uncle?'

She could have retorted, No more than Liza is. You are dangerous; for all I know you could be wicked. But that girl has never seen you as an uncle any more than I could.

She pretended to laugh, but she knew she must watch what she said, because she was so vulnerable that too sharp a reply could have shattered her. To the other passengers they made a striking couple, the tall, hawk-faced man who seemed vaguely familiar, and the cool blonde. They talked, and often the girl smiled, and no one could guess how wretched she was feeling.

They talked more on this journey than they had done going out, and all of it was amicable. She could have been a casual fellow passenger on whom he had no future designs at all. He was good and charming company, but there was no intimacy between them now.

Going out, they had touched all the time, or perhaps it had seemed that way because she had been so sensually aware. But now, like a courteous stranger, he kept his distance.

In the car from the airport the radio played—news and a discussion group—and it was dark when they reached her home town. She recognised nobody in the streets, and she doubted if anyone recognised her.

He drew up in front of her house and brought the cases to the door while she opened it. In the hall she turned on lights, picked up yesterday's mail—two letters lying on the floor—and asked, 'Are you putting your car away?'

'Later.'

There had been lights on at house windows and a street-lamp not far from her front door. She would be surprised if they hadn't been spotted, and by now somebody had probably worked out that they had gone away together.

'The gossips could be having a field-day,' she said, and he shrugged.

'If that embarrasses you, say I gave you a lift somewhere and picked you up again on the way back.' Not many would believe that, but it didn't matter. The house seemed so empty that she didn't want him to leave her, and as he went towards the stairs she said hesitantly, 'Will you come down again? Or could I come up to you?'

'No,' he said, with no hesitation at all. 'I've got work to do and I'm sure you have. I'll see you tomorrow.'

She went into her bed-sit, not looking back, and closing the door behind her. She had asked for that second rejection, laid herself open to it, when any moron could see that he had wearied of her.

He probably would see her tomorrow as they were living in the same house, but he was making it plain that from now she could go back to the wimps because, as far as he was concerned, the game was not worth the candle.

She looked at the two letters she held—one envelope was typed, the other handwritten—and took them with her into the office, where she sat down at her desk and switched on the answerphone. She was in no hurry to hear the messages, but she needed to fill the silence.

Ros from the estate agents came on first. She and Jason had really enjoyed running into Alice and Ivan at the Five Crosses, and how about making a foursome some other night? Not with Ivan, thought Alice. He will be going nowhere with me.

Next was Martin; would she ring him? Then a long-distance friend wanting a chat. After her there was a local friend who had heard the Robin and Martin gossip and wanted to know what was going on—and she was well behind the times. Next was a girl who said she'd try again later. Then there was a second call from Martin, beginning to sound peevish.

The last call was from the couple who were starting up as interior design consultants, and Maxine—of Maxine and Max—was bubbling with excitement because they had been asked to look over the home of Felicity Kerr. 'She's on TV; if we got a commission from her we could get some publicity out of that, couldn't we?' Would Alice phone them?

She had to be Ivan's ex. Her name was Felicity. And he had told Alice he knew a young TV actress who had just bought a house not far from here and who might be interested in the service Maxine and Max had to offer.

'Please ask her,' Alice had said, and it seemed he had; and even if she was his ex she was willing to take his advice.

She tapped out their number and got Max, and said that this sounded interesting, and when would they be going over?

'Tomorrow morning,' he said.

'And where is the house?' He gave her the address and she said, 'I might see you there, but good luck anyway.'

She had seen Felicity Kerr in a couple of TV plays. She was gorgeous and a good actress. Going over to meet her in the flesh might be a rotten idea, but she knew she was going, and that the sickness creeping over her was jealousy.

She had had her first taste of that when Liza Le Breton threw herself into Ivan's arms, but Felicity had been his woman, and if she let herself dwell on what that meant she would be torn apart.

Probably his woman. Felicity was not that uncommon a name. He could know two of them. But she had to meet this one, and any appointments she had for Monday morning would have to wait.

Last Monday she had lunched with Ivan in the precinct, and jumped like a scalded cat when he touched her hand as she reached for the bill. Just one week ago, and now she was desperate for his touch.

Everything had happened at a dizzying rate, but they should never have stopped; they should have become lovers. Possessing her physically could not have given him more power over her than he already had, nor left her more defenceless.

He didn't know that; he probably wouldn't care much if he did. If he had really wanted her he wouldn't have given up because she seemed to be playing games. But she wanted him as if her life depended on it, and she might still have time to undo the damage of the night of the Valentine Ball.

Although when she remembered how Felicity Kerr had looked she knew that, if the actress was a rival, Alice herself stood about as much chance as one of Granny Rosa's racing tips.

CHAPTER EIGHT

FELICITY KERR'S new home was a new house in a nearby town. Max's van was parked in the road and Ivan's Jaguar stood in the drive.

Alice had heard him drive away from outside her house last night, but she had not heard him come back. He could have used the iron staircase to his apartment or he could just as easily have stayed here.

He was certainly here now, and she was beginning to wish that she was not. But Maxine was waving from a window—Alice's car was conspicuous with its question mark logo—so she had to go in.

She took a few moments to compose herself. She might not be all that beautiful, but she could usually manage to look cool, and she took deep, steadying breaths and hoped she could carry off the part of a successful career woman.

This was work. These were her clients. Even if she could be ragingly jealous of the customer and confused out of her mind over the man.

The door was slightly ajar and she called, 'May I come in?'

They were all in a big room leading off the hall. The furniture was spaced out and sparse: a big squashy sofa, chairs, a bureau, a couple of Indian rugs on the wood-block floor. The walls were white, and over the mock-fireplace with its gas flame fire was a dramatic poster-sized black and white photograph of the actress.

In the flesh she was even more fantastic. Her eyes were an incredible blue, her skin was golden-bronze, smooth and shining, and her hair hung in a thick plait almost to her waist.

She was wearing leather trousers and a black blouse knotted at the front, showing a midriff of flawlessly tanned skin. The tan obviously went all over, and just looking at her made Alice feel anaemic.

Ivan stood by the fireplace, looking at home—but he always looked at home—and Maxine and Max were their usual selves, small and wiry and enthusiastic. Alice had known them both for some time, and if anyone could make a success of their new venture, Flair on a Shoe-string, they could.

'You're the landlady?' said Felicity Kerr, having given Alice an up-and-down inspection.

Alice supposed she was talking about the house Alice shared with Ivan and said, 'No, I just have the downstairs flat.'

'We tried to phone you a couple of times over the weekend Alice, but you weren't in,' said Maxine. 'Were you doing anything interesting?'

Alice found her eyes swivelling towards Ivan. When she'd entered the room she had not even acknowledged him. He was standing a little apart from the others, and she had gone towards them. But she was still more conscious of him than of anyone else here, even the vibrant young actress.

Now in one swift glance she knew that he was expecting her to say something like, Nothing much. He thought she would be too embarrassed to tell the truth, and her predicament amused him.

A touch of temper that she never knew she had made her words come quick and bright. 'Oh, I went

to Jersey on Friday, with Ivan. We came back
yesterday.'

She knew then for sure that Felicity had been, or
was, much more than a friend, because the eyes
blazed. Eyes were surely never that blue naturally; they
had to be contact lenses.

'Very pleasant, Jersey, this time of year,' said Ivan,
and Felicity rolled her blue, blue eyes, then laughed
as if Alice was no competition at all.

Maxine and Max had probably been more taken
aback than Felicity, and Maxine rushed in to bridge
the awkward moment, saying what all of them knew.
'Ivan put a word in for us; wasn't that kind of him?'

'Thank you,' said Alice.

'Thank *you*,' Felicity echoed gaily. 'The house is
taking most of my capital, so Flair on a Shoe-string
sounds about right.'

'Well, I'll leave you to it,' said Ivan, and Felicity
put a hand on his arm.

'You can't go; I need your advice. Please.' She
smiled imploringly at him, and Alice knew that this
might be Felicity's house but she was expecting Ivan
to share it.

'Do you have a house?' Max was asking him.

'Just a fisherman's cottage in Cornwall. Two up,
two down, and full of my junk.'

'There's not much scope there, so we're concen-
trating here,' said Felicity, and it was stupid for Alice
to feel a pang because she would never see the cottage.
'Now, we need a study. One of the rooms upstairs.
And I do have ideas for the bedroom. Shall we go
up?'

Alice didn't want to go too; nobody suggested she
should. She was not the house design expert, and the

last thing she wanted to hear was Felicity Kerr's plans for her bedroom. Walking into the bedroom would be enough to throw Alice right off keel. She was none too steady as it was.

If they were up there long she would call up, Sorry, I have to go; I'll be in touch, and get the heck out of here. She shouldn't have come. She had wanted to see Felicity, but she hadn't bargained on seeing her with Ivan. That had managed to knock the stuffing out of Alice, and she flopped down on the sofa, limp as a rag doll.

He would work in the study, of course, and share the bedroom, and this house would become a place to come home to. It was without any sort of character so far, but Maxine and Max would change that. They would build up an atmosphere, scout around for furniture and fittings. But I'll bet she won't be collecting chipped mugs from car boot sales, Alice thought wryly, as the black and white photograph looked scornfully down at her.

A week ago, exchanging confidences of a sort with him, Alice had got the impression that the girl who answered to Felicity wanted a commitment that he did not. But he was still moving in with her, as a partner, a lover, and when he took off on his travels he would come back to her.

She was an actress, she must get around too, but this house would be their trysting place, and Alice wished she had never set eyes on it.

Felicity came running down the stairs and gave Alice a none too friendly stare. 'You still here? What are you *doing* here?'

She was at the bureau, getting a page torn from a magazine, and Alice said, 'I handle their publicity.'

'Oh!' That changed her attitude. She considered briefly, then called from the bottom of the stairs. 'Ellen's interviewing me; I won't be long.'

Ellen? She hadn't even registered Alice's name. She sat down beside Alice on the sofa, her blue eyes suddenly shrewd and calculating. 'Now how are you handling this?'

Fine, thought Alice. You want publicity and so do they, and I must start doing my job. She said, 'Well, they're just starting off, and you are their ideal client. You're young, you're with it, and you also happen to be famous.'

Felicity was more starlet than star, but she accepted 'famous' with a smug little smile as Alice went on, 'They're good, they really are, and prices don't come any sharper. If they were advising you on your home I could get a picture and copy in the locals for starters. What are you doing now? Anything with a local angle?'

Felicity was starting next month in a TV three-parter, some of the filming taking place in an ancestral pile not too far away. Alice made notes and Felicity smiled smugly again. 'I'm lucky; I do seem to get the parts. Best of all, one of Ivan's books is being filmed, and he wrote a lovely part in it specially for me.'

'Which book?' Alice asked, and this time Felicity gave her a brilliant smile.

'I don't want that mentioned just yet. I'd better get back; do you want to hear what they're suggesting for us up there?'

'No, thank you,' Alice said hastily. 'I have another appointment. I'll be in touch about the photographs.'

'Do that.' Felicity went with her to the front door, and as she held it open she said softly, 'You seem a nice enough girl, and he's a helluva man.' And there was pity tinged with contempt in her expression. 'But don't even dream of it,' she said as she closed the door.

Alice went home first, worked for a while, and skipped lunch before she set off for the market. She couldn't eat at the deli, her usual Monday treat, because she would be remembering Ivan sitting opposite and wouldn't be able to swallow for the lump in her throat.

Passing Patsy's shop in the precinct was bad enough, and when Patsy came hurrying out Alice almost ran. Patsy wanted to talk about the opening again, how well it had gone, and what a smashing picture they had had in today's *Herald*. And wasn't Ivan Blackmore something?'

'Yes, he is,' said Alice. 'I'm in rather a rush.'

'Oh, and Granny Rosa said if I saw you to ask if you backed her tip on Saturday, because it won.'

Alice laughed at that, and managed to keep smiling at the right times as she went from stall to stall, gathering her copy.

Keeping busy got her through the afternoon, but when she returned home the phone was ringing. She picked it up and Maxine shrilled, 'Alice, did you really go away with him for the weekend?'

'Yes,' said Alice. She could hardly deny something she had announced so flatly.

'Well, she isn't going to give him up in a hurry,' said Maxine, sounding worried for her friend, 'so don't get in too deep.'

Don't even dream . . .

'I won't,' said Alice. 'How did it go this morning?'

It had gone quite well. They had discussed plans and terms, and Felicity Kerr looked like being their first celebrity client.

'Splendid,' said Alice. 'I hope they'll be very happy there.' She put down the phone quite gently. Then she took a pencil out of the top drawer of her desk and snapped it in two.

She had no real grounds for grievance. Ivan had never promised that an affair with Alice would mean his forsaking all others. He had said Felicity was an ex, but yesterday's ex could be today's lover again, and it did show how little Alice really counted.

Never mind the game she was supposed to be playing. He was certainly fooling with her, and the awful thing was that for most of the time he had seemed like everything she would need for the rest of her life.

That was her mistake. Not leading him on and letting him down. Anger was what she was feeling now, not hurt or jealousy.

She had nearly been taken for a ride, when he must have intended going round to Felicity's last night or this morning. Whatever had happened on Valentine night, he would probably still have done that, and she was glad now that she had panicked.

A chastity belt of terror was something she had to thank the intruder for. That was a sickening thought, but it chilled her blazing anger down to a slow burn and it put the steel back in her spine. She hoped he would stay at Felicity's. A pair of high achievers, they had plenty in common, and Alice would find life easier if he was no longer under her roof.

She must get on with her work and keep him out of her mind, and she did work, fast and with her usual competence, until she saw him pass the French windows, going towards the iron staircase.

Then she jumped up, because there was something she had to say to him. She was not quite sure what, but it was urgent enough to have her flinging the doors open and reaching the bottom of the staircase before he was at the top. 'When are you moving in?' she heard herself call.

'What?' He stopped and looked down.

'With Felicity.'

'That doesn't concern you.' He went in through the door at the top and she ran up after him. They were in what had been Miss Pringle's kitchen, where he had cooked spaghetti marinara for her, and if there had been a pan of it simmering on the stove she might well have picked it up and thrown it at him.

'That's right,' she raged. 'It isn't my business, but you were going to her, weren't you, as soon as you got back from Jersey?'

'Yes.'

'So it's as well that little trip ended on a platonic note. Not that anybody's going to believe that.'

'If you didn't want them knowing you shouldn't have told them,' he said, as if any idiot could have worked that out, and the long mouth quirked cynically. 'But the men in your life won't find it hard to believe that even when you were prancing around naked you were still saying "Hands off".'

He went out of the kitchen, shutting the door, and she screamed her silent scream, because there was no answer to that. Coming back down the iron staircase, she nearly fell, grabbing the rail and hanging on, panting as if she had been running for miles. She was still breathless at her desk, and she sat back and forced herself into a semblance of calm until it became the real thing.

That had been a bad experience, and if she couldn't forget it she would have to live with it. She had had practice there. She had to go on now, doing her job, meeting her friends, playing it cool.

The work she could do, because she was used to it and good at it. The friends were harder to handle, because that week everybody she met seemed to want to hear about her weekend away with Ivan Blackmore.

She told them all, 'Yes, we went. Why not? We're neighbours, friends, but beyond that there is nothing going on.' Some might have believed her, some didn't, and Martin arrived on her doorstep on Thursday gibbering with indignation.

She had made him look a complete fool, right after he had announced their engagement. 'What engagement?' she said. 'I always told you no.'

'Are you serious about this man?'

'I've hardly spoken to him in days. It was never serious. It was never anything.'

'I just don't know where I am with you,' Martin said, adding, 'And Mother's changing her mind about us being right for each other.'

'Listen to Mother,' Alice said. 'You always do.'

She had spoken to Ivan. They were in the same house. When they met in the hallway she said, 'Hello,' and he replied with a few good-humoured words, and it was exactly as she had said—neighbours and no more.

Which was what she wanted, of course. She was not getting involved with him again, but she knew

when he was up there. Especially at night. As she lay
in bed when everything else was quiet she could sometimes hear footsteps, the sound of music and sometimes not, and what the silence meant was none of
her concern, but those were the nights she found it
harder to get to sleep.

It had been a busy week. Among other things she
had persuaded the home page editor of a monthly
magazine to feature Maxine and Max and how they
proposed giving the young actress style on a budget.

On Friday afternoon she phoned through to tell
them, and Maxine said that was brilliant. Any time
that suited the editor was OK by them. 'How's it
working out?' Alice asked.

'It isn't all sweetness and light,' said Maxine. 'She's
a bit of a cow when he's not around.'

Felicity Kerr had not struck Alice as a sweetie. She
asked, 'Can you handle it?' and Maxine said breezily,

'Sure; she wants good service on the cheap, and
that's us.'

'Is—is he there much?'

'No, worse luck,' said Maxine.

That was interesting. Alice considered that all over
the weekend while she was out with friends, talking
about everything but Ivan Blackmore, and by Sunday
night she thought she had come to a sensible
conclusion.

She knew, and Ivan must know now, that there
would be strings to him moving in with Felicity, and
he was restless to his bones, and it could be that he
didn't want anyone building a nest for him.

He could have gone there before, instead of taking
a lease on Miss Pringle's flat, so why change his mind
now? He had never said he had. It was Felicity who

had given that impression. 'Don't even dream of it', she had said, but why should Alice listen to Felicity?

After nearly a week she could see no reason why she should not make the first move towards easing the situation between herself and Ivan. Why shouldn't they be friends again? The first chance she got she would tell him Granny Rosa's horse had romped home, and that he had an invitation from the witch in Patsy's family to visit a genuine Romany vardo.

He might be intrigued. At least it would get them talking, and from then on she would go as slowly as she should have gone before.

She left home early on Monday morning, for a conference on a future promotion drive a car hire firm was holding at a local hotel, and came back in the late afternoon.

The door at the top of the stairs was open, and as she dumped her briefcase she decided that this was the time. If there was anyone with him—of course she meant Felicity—they would surely have closed the connecting door. She took off her coat and hung it in the hall closet.

Remember Granny Rosa? she was going to start, and she had a foot on the bottom step when he appeared at the top. 'I was just coming up,' she said.

'I'll save you the trouble. I'm coming down.'

She licked lips that were suddenly dry, letting him get into the hall. He might have been going to pass her without stopping to ask what she wanted, but she was determined to have her say. Only he asked, 'How do you feel about going up in a balloon?'

Her face went blank and stupid. 'What?'

'The silver balloon won a prize. There was a letter this morning.'

It would be addressed to him—he had made the booking and settled the account—but she couldn't believe her luck. She said, 'I don't believe it.'

'Do you want it?'

'For two? In a real balloon?' Of course it was; they could hardly go up tied to a toy one. He nodded and she beamed.

'That is something I have always wanted to do.'

She had told him that, but he had probably forgotten, and this was the most incredibly lucky break. She had never ever won a raffle before. Better than a trip to the vardo any day, a flight in a balloon would be an adventure that must blow most of the troubles away. 'You would come?' she asked.

'Why not?'

'I would love that. When?'

'How are you for Wednesday?'

'This Wednesday? The day after tomorrow?'

'Weather permitting, we can take a flight from Long Logan airfield. They've had a cancellation.'

This was magic. How could anything work out this smoothly? But she wasn't questioning, just going for it and thanking her stars. Her mind raced over her appointments for Wednesday, and there seemed to be nothing that couldn't be rearranged. 'What time?' she said.

'The flight's scheduled for nine in the morning. If we leave here at eight that should give us plenty of time.'

She was thrilled to bits. She babbled, 'You know, I've never won a thing before in my whole life. It's the Granny Rosa syndrome, because her horse won on Saturday, and that's got to be a first too. This has been a week of consolation prizes for losers.'

He smiled at her. 'Let's hope the weather holds.'

'Oh, it will.' He left her smiling, and she started right away fixing a free day for herself. She would work tonight and tomorrow, and she phoned to postpone a couple of appointments. When she explained she had a chance to go up in a balloon which she didn't want to miss, they were both understanding, especially the one who knew about Ivan Blackmore; she had quite a chat with her.

On Tuesday evening she did the paperwork and went to bed early; she wanted to be fresh and bright in the morning. When she'd seen Ivan in the hall that day she'd asked, 'It's still on?'

'Yes, so far.'

She'd hugged herself, because surely nothing could go wrong when she had such high hopes, and early morning was fine with a little breeze blowing. Perfect weather, just as she had known it would be.

She pinned the Mizpah brooch to her sweater. 'The Lord watch over thee and me when we are absent one from the other'. And she prayed, Watch over us when we are together, and please make things right between us.

When Ivan came downstairs at eight o'clock she was near the bottom of the stairs, wrapped up in jeans, sweater and fleecy-lined jacket, asking him, 'Shall I be warm enough?'

'Too warm, probably. The burners give out a good heat and you don't feel the wind; you're riding it.'

So she changed her jacket for a lambswool cardigan, and they left the house to walk round to where his car was garaged. She slipped her hand through his arm, and from across the road Karen Morton gave them a cool nod. Alice was exuberant enough to find that funny, and she called a cheery, 'Hi there, Karen.'

In the car it was almost like last weekend when they were driving away together, although this morning he didn't tell her she was beautiful, nor touch her face in a caress.

But it was good, and she enjoyed every minute of the ten-mile journey to the wartime airport that was now an aviation club for light aircraft and gliders, with the balloon centre well clear of the buildings.

Parking the car, they met the pilot, who was wearing an old leather flying jacket, and joined a middle-aged man with a boy, plainly his son, and a youngish couple who looked apprehensive and were holding hands tightly, in the wicker basket.

The padded sides came up to Alice's chest, and she held on to the side and leaned back against Ivan as the valves were turned on with a blast, and gas ignited, warming the air. Then a high jet of flame roared into the centre of the heap of billowing canvas, which inflated above them into a huge multi-coloured balloon, straining against the ropes that were holding it down.

As they drifted slowly upwards Alice scanned the scene below—the moving figures of the ground crew, a car that had just drawn up and the man who jumped out. He stood, looking up, and she yelped, 'That's Martin.'

She could see him well enough to recognise him, and she was glad he hadn't arrived before because, although he couldn't have stopped her and he probably wouldn't have tried, he was a nuisance she did not want around.

Ivan asked, 'Did you tell him?'

'No, but he could have heard about it.'

Obviously he had, and she hoped he would not hang about for their return. 'I don't know what he thinks he's doing,' she said.

All the other passengers were too busy taking photographs to hear or care what Alice was saying, and she thought, I must remember it all, every single detail, as Martin and all her stresses slipped from her mind, leaving her revelling in the lovely floating feeling, like being on a cloud, going with the wind.

When they came to a fir plantation a burst on the burners sent them zooming higher, with the tops of the tall trees scraping the bottom of the basket. Sounds drifted up. She heard the squeal of a motorcyclist's brakes on a bend of a country lane, the mooing of cows from far below. The balloon stayed high; low flying spooked the animals and the more sensitive citizens, the pilot told them.

It was fun spotting places she knew and pointing them out to Ivan, but nobody talked much. It was so peaceful, so relaxing, the only disturbance the occasional swoosh of the burners. Sometimes she smiled blissfully at Ivan, and his arm around her shoulders was light and companionable. Not lover-like. He *could* have been an uncle with a favourite niece, but at least they were friendly again, and that was something to build on in the weeks ahead.

After the scheduled hour's flight another half-hour floated by looking for a landing spot, a big enough field away from buildings and power cables, with no animals and no sign of crops.

The landing was made with the tiniest of bumps, and then they had to wait while the pilot contacted the men in the retrieval van on his mobile phone. They

would get in touch with the landowner for permission
to disembark. Within minutes the van was coming up
the farm track and bouncing across the field. But it
was long enough for a sightseeing group of two men,
three women, four children and a dog to have
gathered.

While the balloon was being deflated and stowed
into a bag, everything being packed into the van,
champagne was produced, glasses poured, and a
miniature birthday cake presented to the boy; the flight
had been a present for his sixteenth birthday.

Alice was loving it. She drank her champagne in a
swinging party mood. She could have stayed longer
in the field, sipping champagne with these nice people
with whom she had just shared a red-letter day. But
it was into the van, and the adventure was almost over.

She never thought about Martin again until they
drove through the entrance to the aviation club, and
then she looked to see if his car had gone. It was not
where she had seen it when the balloon took off, but
it was parked with the others, and Martin was at the
wheel.

Ivan followed her gaze, and she met his eyes. 'Do
you want to go back with him?' he asked quietly.

'Of course not.'

As they climbed out of the van Martin began to
walk towards them, and Ivan said, 'Wait here,' and
went to meet him. The other passengers were still on
a high from the thrill of the flight, thanking the pilot,
planning to book again before long. Alice saw Ivan
take Martin's arm and turn him back towards the
parked cars. Much the taller man, Ivan bent his head
slightly, and what he said was spoken too softly to
reach her.

But it reached Martin, who got into the car, apparently without protest, and drove off. Alice joined the chorus of goodbyes and climbed into the passenger seat as Ivan opened the door for her. Then she asked, 'What did you say to him?'

'I said I'd see you back.'

'You must have been persuasive.'

He grinned. 'If you will choose wimps, you can't expect them to withstand pressure.'

'Well, nobody could accuse Felicity of being a wimp,' she said immediately.

'I don't think anyone ever has.'

He was smiling, but in profile his was a hard face, the jawline clean and the mouth strong and sensual. She said, 'So one of your books is being filmed?'

'Yes.'

'And you wrote a part in it for Felicity.'

'Who told you that?'

'She did.'

He laughed. 'Did she, now?' And that was all she was getting on that, because he steered the talk back to the balloon flight and for the rest of the journey she relived it again, chattering away, because she had enjoyed herself immensely.

He drew up outside their house and said, 'You might as well get out; I'll garage the car.'

'What are you doing then?'

'Working.'

He meant it. There was no indecision. So that was the end of their time together today, and all she could do was smile and say, 'Well, it was wonderful,' and get out of the car and let herself into the house.

They had left before the mail arrived this morning, and she picked up a circular, a phone bill and a large envelope. She looked at the name of the hotel printed on the envelope, then opened it.

A silk scarf, in a checkerboard pattern of purple, green and yellow, fell out. She read the letter that came with it and then sat on the bottom of the stairs to read it again.

When Ivan walked into the hall ten minutes later she was still sitting there. 'I thought my luck had changed,' she said, 'but this is ridiculous.'

'What are you talking about?'

She handed him the letter and held up the scarf. '*Two* prizes with one silver balloon?'

He grinned. 'How was I to know we were on to a winner?'

'*You* booked today's trip. You had to have booked it.' She had worked that out, but what it must mean was making her dizzy.

'You said you wanted to go up in a balloon, and I know the crew who run the centre.' He was a man with contacts; there wouldn't be much he couldn't fix. 'I asked if they'd let me have the first cancellation, and we were lucky there; one came up.'

'Why didn't you tell me?'

He shrugged. 'I doubted if you'd go if you knew I'd bought the tickets.' She had made a fuss about being independent, and lately there had been the coolness between them, but now she was delighted that he had done this for her. 'Besides,' he added cheerfully, 'a balloon trip for the silver balloon sounded fairly reasonable.'

She had accepted that. She hadn't bothered about credibility; she had grabbed at it. She was still sitting on the bottom of the stairs, looking up at the tall man.

'Well, thank you,' she said gravely. 'It was a lovely present.'

'I'm glad.'

He sounded as if this could have been a treat for a favourite niece, and she stood up, her voice truly serious now, asking him, 'Please, do come in and let's—talk.'

He shook his head slightly. 'Better not, I'm trying not to make the same mistakes again, but it isn't easy.'

He passed her and went up the stairs, and a little frown drew her brows together, creasing the smooth forehead. What mistakes? He had to mean getting involved with her, but if saying no to her wasn't easy there had to be a chink in his armour.

She followed. He was in the living-room, and she stood in the open doorway. 'Please will you listen to me?' she said. 'There is something I have to tell you.'

He was listening, waiting, and she took a few steps into the room before she could blurt out, 'I don't tease. I wasn't playing games. I was scared to death.'

He said incredulously, 'Of me? For God's sake, *why*?'

She was standing where her bed had been and he was at the window, and her voice was a whisper, 'The break-in, before my father died. Ros talked about it.'

'I remember that you didn't make much of it.'

'No, but it wasn't quite how Ros remembered. It was only one man, with a Balaclava over his head, and he ripped my nightdress off.' Her shoulders were hunched, her arms crossed over her breasts, and she found herself beginning to rock slightly to and fro. 'He came in through that window. I was here in bed, and he gagged me and tied my wrists to the bedposts.'

Somehow Ivan's arms were around her. 'I couldn't tell anyone,' she said. 'My father's heart was weak; he died of a heart attack less than two years after, so I didn't help him much, but I couldn't distress him. I had to—laugh it off.'

She could feel sick hysterical laughter welling up, and he said, 'Tell me what happened to you,' and the hysteria died down.

She spoke with her face pressed hard against his chest, muffling her voice. 'I didn't know that my father and his friends were coming back. I didn't think that anyone would come back for hours. I couldn't move or scream, and all the time I could hear him moving round the house, and I knew how he was going to hurt me; I thought he was going to kill me, and I could feel it happening.'

She was shaking from head to foot, but he was rock-steady and she clung to him until she could speak again, although she was almost sobbing now.

'I couldn't tell anyone, and after my father died it was too late, but I've been terrified ever since of being in any man's power. He said he'd be back. I know he won't—that's a crazy idea—but I couldn't forget it, and I was frightened of you because you made me feel helpless again.'

He still held her in silence for a moment. Then he said, 'You'll never be helpless with me. I'll always be on your side.'

She felt his strength flowing into her like a cleansing current healing her. She gulped in his breath and the coolness of his skin, and it was as though she had been very ill, but now she was free from poison and soon she would hardly remember the sickness.

On the sofa he cradled her against him, gently stroking her hair, and when she looked up he said, 'I should have gone slowly. We will now. I'd decided on that anyway.'

Before she had told him anything that was how she had planned it herself. They had rushed into an intimate relationship, but this time there need be no hurry. She closed her eyes and let his fingers move through her hair, brushing the nape of her neck, circling the top of her spinal column with feather-light pressure.

But the shock from that ran all the way down her spine and shot off, tingling, into most of her nerve-ends. Never mind about erotic zones. Anywhere was an erotic zone. Just looking up into his face made her feel like a flower opening in the sun.

She wanted him. She felt that she would wither away if she didn't have him. She was still in sweater and cardigan, and she got out of the cardigan and began to pull her sweater over her head. 'Is this a good idea?' he said.

'Do you want me?'

'Of course I want you.' His voice was controlled, his eyes hooded. 'But we have done this before, and, although I understand better now, it would be hellish if it happened again.'

'Not this time,' she said. She leaned towards him and he put his arms around her, unfastening the clasp of her bra so that she was naked to the waist. Then she took off his jacket, his tie, his shirt, and her hands were trembling.

She fumbled with her waistband and he slid her skirt down. 'Nothing you don't want to do,' he said, but her senses were swimming. There was nothing she didn't want to do. She wanted to do everything, with him. She lay back with a little moan, and he was handling her as if she were porcelain, with a delicate touching of hands and lips, slowly, slowly, all the caresses a stroking sensual delight.

When he ran fingertips lingeringly down the sides of her breasts from armpits to hipbones and across she could feel the arousal building up in her, the hunger rising. She was shuddering, gasping, and he feathered a kiss across her lips, sending streaking fire through her veins, and said huskily, 'We can stop any time.'

She raised his head, her fingers gripping fiercely through the thick, unruly hair, looking into dark, wild eyes. 'Is that a fact?' she said, and he laughed without sound.

'No, it is not,' he said, and she laughed aloud as they rolled, locked together, from the sofa on to the floor.

She had no mind left and her body was out of control. She had never known such ecstasy existed anywhere in the world. Every nerve, every cell, every drop of blood in her was singing and sobbing. Bite and scratch, and cling and kiss, riding faster and faster, as though she rode a wild horse, feeling the ripple of muscles beneath her skin, under her skin. And then the tiger turned on her, and she was a tigress, and the fighting was loving, gripping and straining, and an incredibly piercing fusion was taking her down to the depths and up beyond the heights, and like a litany she could hear herself sobbing then screaming, 'Yes,' and, 'Yes, yes, *yes* . . .'

Minutes or hours later she opened her eyes and met his eyes again. They lay side by side, one of his arms lay across her, and he propped himself up on an elbow.

He was a marvellous man in his sinewy muscle power; she could have lain here looking at him for hours. Her limbs felt heavy, as if she had just run a marathon, and in a way she guessed she had done something of the sort, riding the rapids and scaling the mountain. She was wrung out, exhausted, but filled with such well-being and happiness that she could have burst out singing if only she'd had the strength.

'All right?' he said.

'Righter than right.' She was still breathless.

'That's as well,' he said, 'because you've done it now; I don't think I'll ever get enough of you.' He lifted a lock of hair from her damp forehead and his touch stirred her senses again, taking the tiredness away.

He said, 'I told myself it didn't matter when I thought you were playing games. I walked the beaches that night and I thought I could handle it, but I seem to have been in deep over you from the beginning.'

And she heard herself asking a question she had never asked. 'Do you love me?' Others had told her they loved her without being asked, but now her heart stopped beating while she waited, and although he answered almost at once it seemed a long time.

He spoke slowly, 'Yes, I love you, and I've never said that to anyone before.'

'Not to Felicity?'

'We were lovers, but I never said I loved her.'

He sounded surprised, realising this, and she couldn't remember ever saying, I love you, to anyone either. I'm very fond of you, was what she had used to say, but this was love she felt for him, total and enduring, and she could smile as she teased, 'Were you moving in with Felicity?'

She sat up, curling up against him, and he said, 'I never even considered that, but it was when you asked when I was that I knew I could never walk away from you. I phoned the balloon centre that day, and I was not going to rush things this time. I was all set for the waiting game and just keeping the competition back.'

She couldn't hold back a giggle. 'Like Martin? Was that all you said to him—that you were seeing me home?'

'I may have mentioned what I'd do to him if he didn't get the hell out of it.' Spoken softly, with that menacing look of steely strength, it had been quite enough to see Martin off. Martin might try to warn her against this dangerous man, but he would not be arriving on her doorstep again.

'You're a thug,' she said cheerfully, and he considered that.

'Possibly, but I'm your thug.'

'Every woman should have a thug on her side.'

She put her hands on his shoulders, and her laughter died in her throat as he cupped her face in his hands and breathed her name, 'Alice,' so that it sounded like a poem or a prayer. 'I'm not often at a loss for words,' he said. 'I love you, which means I want you with me every hour of the day and night. You are . . .' He hesitated, then he said, 'Another small word I've never used before—my wife?'

The inflexion made it a question, which it was not, because he was her man, her lover, her husband. 'Will you marry me?' he said.

'Of course.'

'Yes,' he said, 'of course.'

They smiled at each other, their faces so close that looking into his eyes almost sent her cross-eyed. She said, 'And Granny Rosa said we were chalk and cheese, a travelling man and a homebody.'

'It's good to be home, wherever you are,' he said.

'And I'll go where you go.'

'Together' was another small word that promised a lifetime's joy. They had turned Miss Pringle's living-room into their lair, and wherever they went the magic would hold.

The look in his eyes she had seen on the beach. She hadn't recognised it then, but she did now. It was naked commitment, and they had wasted a whole week, and she said ruefully, 'I would have explained that night if you'd stayed in the shower.'

His grin was wicked. 'If I hadn't got out and got covered you'd have seen the effect you were having on me, and at the time I thought that would give you an unfair advantage.'

She laughed and stood up and went into the bathroom, turning on the shower and stepping under the cascading water. With shining eyes in a smiling face, she held out wet, shining arms, inviting, 'Join me?'

'Any time, anywhere,' he said, and did.

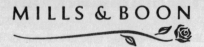

MILLS & BOON

Proudly present...

CHARLOTTE LAMB'S
♥ 100th ♥
ROMANCE

This is a remarkable achievement for a writer who had her
first Mills & Boon novel published in 1973. Some six million
words later and with sales around the world, her novels
continue to be popular with romance fans everywhere.

Her centenary romance '*VAMPIRE LOVER*' is a suspense-
filled story of dark desires and tangled emotions—Charlotte
Lamb at her very best.

Published: June 1994   Price: £1.90

Next Month's Romances

Each month you can choose from a wide variety of romance with Mills & Boon. Below are the new titles to look out for next month, why not ask either Mills & Boon Reader Service or your Newsagent to reserve you a copy of the titles you want to buy – just tick the titles you would like and either post to Reader Service or take it to any Newsagent and ask them to order your books.

Please save me the following titles: Please tick ✓

PASSIONATE OPPONENT	Jenny Cartwright	
AN IMPOSSIBLE DREAM	Emma Darcy	
SHATTERED WEDDING	Elizabeth Duke	
A STRANGER'S KISS	Liz Fielding	
THE FURY OF LOVE	Natalie Fox	
THE LAST ILLUSION	Diana Hamilton	
DANGEROUS DESIRE	Sarah Holland	
STEPHANIE	Debbie Macomber	
BITTER MEMORIES	Margaret Mayo	
A TASTE OF PASSION	Kristy McCallum	
PHANTOM LOVER	Susan Napier	
WEDDING BELLS FOR BEATRICE	Betty Neels	
DARK VICTORY	Elizabeth Oldfield	
LOVE'S STING	Catherine Spencer	
CHASE A DREAM	Jennifer Taylor	
EDGE OF DANGER	Patricia Wilson	

If you would like to order these books in addition to your regular subscription from Mills & Boon Reader Service please send £1.90 per title to: Mills & Boon Reader Service, Freepost, P.O. Box 236, Croydon, Surrey, CR9 9EL, quote your Subscriber No:..................................... (if applicable) and complete the name and address details below. Alternatively, these books are available from many local Newsagents including W H Smith, J Menzies, Martins and other paperback stockists from 8 July 1994.

Name:...

Address:...

....Post Code:...........................

To Retailer: If you would like to stock M&B books please contact your regular book/magazine wholesaler for details.

You may be mailed with offers from other reputable companies as a result of this application.
If you would rather not take advantage of these opportunities please tick box. ☐

SUMMER SPECIAL!

Four exciting new Romances for the price of three

Each Romance features British heroines and their encounters with dark and desirable Mediterranean men. *Plus, a free Elmlea recipe booklet inside every pack.*

So sit back and enjoy your sumptuous summer reading pack and indulge yourself with the free Elmlea recipe ideas.

Available July 1994   Price £5.70

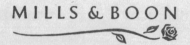

MILLS & BOON

Accept 4 FREE Romances and 2 FREE gifts

FROM READER SERVICE

Here's an irresistible invitation from Mills & Boon. Please accept our offer of 4 FREE Romances, a CUDDLY TEDDY and a special MYSTERY GIFT! Then, if you choose, go on to enjoy 6 captivating Romances every month for just £1.90 each, postage and packing FREE. Plus our FREE Newsletter with author news, competitions and much more.

Send the coupon below to: Mills & Boon Reader Service, FREEPOST, PO Box 236, Croydon, Surrey CR9 9EL.

Yes! Please rush me 4 FREE Romances and 2 FREE gifts! Please also reserve me a Reader Service subscription. If I decide to subscribe I can look forward to receiving 6 brand new Romances for just £11.40 each month, post and packing FREE. If I decide not to subscribe I shall write to you within 10 days - I can keep the free books and gifts whatever I choose. I may cancel or suspend my subscription at any time. I am over 18 years of age.

Ms/Mrs/Miss/Mr _____ EP70R

Address _____

Postcode _____ Signature _____

Offer closes 31st October 1994. The right is reserved to refuse an application and change the terms of this offer. One application per household. Offer not valid for current subscribers to this series. Valid in UK and Eire only. Overseas readers please write for details. Southern Africa write to IBS Private Bag X3010, Randburg 2125. You may be mailed with offers from other reputable companies as a result of this application. Please tick box if you would prefer not to receive such offers ☐

mps
MAILING PREFERENCE SERVICE